Also by Marc Estrin

Novels

And Kings Shall Be Thy Nursing Fathers
The Prison Diaries of Alan Kreiger (Terrorist)
When The God Come Home To Roost
Tsim-Tsum
The Good Doctor Guillotin
Skulk
The Annotated Nose
Goem Song
The Lamentations of Julius Marantz
The Education of Arnold Hitler
Insect Dreams: The Half Life of Gregor Samsa

Memoir

Rehearsing With Gods: Photographs and Essays
on the Bread and Puppet Theater (with Ron Simon,
Photographer)

Speckled Vanities

Marc Estrin

Fomite
Burlington, VT

ISBN-13: 978-1-942515-23-4
Library of Congress Control Number: 2015947753

Fomite
58 Peru Street
Burlington, VT 05401
www.fomitepress.com

Metal sculpture: "Two Heads", by Alexandra Heller
(www.hellerartworks.com)
Photo by Kip Ross (www.kipross.com). Gracious permissions gratefully received. The work evokes for me the longing and fleeing, connections and disconnections at play in the world of the characters. M.E.

And speckled Vanity
Will sicken soon and die,
And leprous Sin will melt from earthly mould;
And Hell itself will pass away,
And leave her dolorous mansions to the peering Day.

> *From*
> *John Milton (1608-74)*
> *On the Morning of Christ's Nativity*

Apolude

Apologies — and homage — to

Cervantes for "The Tale of the Curious Impertinent"
Goethe for *Elective Affinities*
Gustav Mahler for "The Heavenly Life" (Symphony 4)
Bertolt Brecht for *Mahagonny*

Three neighboring locations off Route 95, near Las Vegas, Nevada

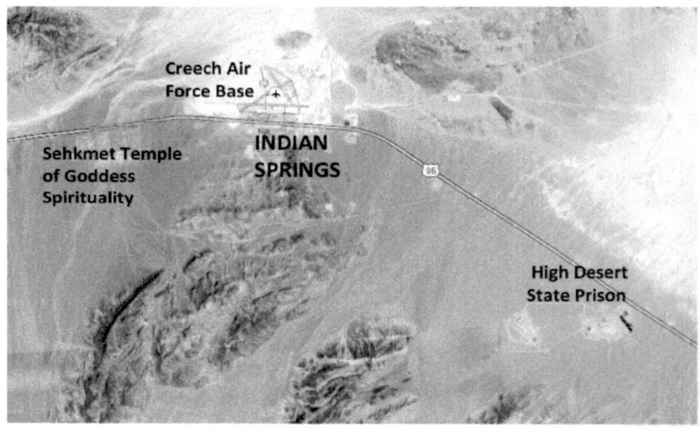

Speckled Vanities

PERFORMANCE

N ever had the best-laid plans of mindful men gone so awry as at the performance of Dido and Aeneas on March 16, 2010 in the gym at the High Desert State Prison (the state's largest), near Indian Springs, Nevada.

Purcell's opera was to be the high point of a visionary joint program combatting violence against women among both inmates at the prison, and soldiers at the neighboring Creech Air Force Base, home to the 432nd Air Expeditionary Wing, the nation's first air base dedicated entirely to unmanned aircraft. Drones in the air, drones at their controls — and drones droning behind bars — all had committed violence against women. Which needed combatting.

Now an opera written in 1689 for the young students of Mr. Josiah Price's Boarding School for Girls in London might seem an odd vehicle with which to explore the personal and systemic urgencies of sexism, chauvinism and deathism. Yet if carefully examined and judiciously performed, it just might do, might uniquely serve the purpose, all threads tied into one revealing pattern, illuminated by evocative music of love and longing, of perfidy and bitterness, of raucous drink and demonic laughter. It might work. Or so they thought.

Aeneas, you may recall, fought bravely at Troy until Hector ordered him to flee with a remnant of Trojans to establish some other Troy overseas, out in the western land. After much blowing around, and many adventures, his sea-gang will end up founding Rome. But on the way, alas, his ship made landfall at Carthage, where Dido, the queen, fell in love with Aeneas, and he with her.

The Hero and the Queen stay and play for a year while witches conspire to destroy them, Carthage, and "all in prosp'rous state" — an objective cheered by many prisoners. In an early COINTEL operation, the Witches send false "orders from Jupiter" demanding that Aeneas get on with his assignment and pack up for Italy. Ordered by the Big Kahuna, what is Aeneas is to do but bid his love adieu and move on?

And herein lay the combined Air Force Base and Prison's projects target — violence against women, and in this case violence against an exemplary Dido whose psychology is laid bare. All to be discussed with the audience after the show.

In an agonizing "How can you do this to me?" scene, Aeneas breaks down, and will stay, no matter the consequences. But Dido will have none of it, will no longer entertain a man who had even once *thought* of leaving her, for whatever reason, for whatever cause, for whatever other god than Love. [The chorus sings "Great Minds against Themselves Conspire".] She forces him out, Aeneas leaves, and Dido dies of disappointment and despair. In one of the most heartrending arias ever composed, she sings "When I am laid in Earth, may my Wrongs create no Trouble in thy Breast. Remember me, remember me, but ah! forget my Fate."

At High Desert State Prison, the prisoners, the soldiers, the guards, the administrative staff, the musicians, the politicians, the reporters, and the small attending public never did get to hear the final lamenting chorus. Why? Because as Dido rent her garments, and as Belinda, her companion, bent over her from behind, revealing a lovely maiden bosom under her stola, one prisoner yelled "Take it off babe, take it off!" and another, empowered by the outburst of the first, stood up in the front row, unzipped his pants, wrestled out an enormous schlong, for some reason musical or other already engorged, jumped up on the platform and invited one or the other woman — or both — to "Suck it, bitch, suck it!"

This was too much for several other prisoners similarly afflicted with priapy, who then rushed the stage, cocks at various angles, battling to get beyond each other at the women, a blue-denim gang, undressing as they went.

Needless to say, this then was too much for the brave men in uniform pledged to protect American women, and to promote family values with unmanned drones. A team of khakis jumped the psychos, and dragged them off the stage. The prison guards, also in khaki, joined the melee against the blues. It was color war! Other blues jumped up to defend their own — not against the guards, who might effect a longterm revenge, but against the faggot khakis who were too shit-scared to actually go to war, and could murder people all day on the other side of the world, and go home to sleep with their wives and take their kids to soccer practice — and not be caught or indicted. And then there were the whites on the browns and the browns on the blacks and the blacks on the whites. And finally, the Sailors on the Witches and vice versa.

In clouds of tear gas, some in the audience tried

to make for the doors, but their way was blocked by fallen folding chairs, and then fallen fleers, and they would have found the doors locked anyway, if only to ensure an audience for the Q&A discussion.

When concluding his introductory talk before the show, Peter Warden had asked the prisoners to please shut off their cell phones (laughter), and politely asked those armed not to shoot Captain Boynton, the piano player. (No laughter.)

Nevertheless, about two minutes into the riot, a shot rang out from someone licensed to carry a gun — or who had otherwise obtained one — and a bullet cracked the dry brown wood of the upright and howled across the strings. Another shot splintered the instrument and sent the harp screaming, snapping, and tearing. Bruce fell to the floor, his retro-black-plastic glasses clattering on ahead of him, the piano player, shot.

The closing line was not "Here keep your watch, and never, never, never part," but "LOCK IT! LOCK IT DOWN! LOCK IT THE FUCK DOWN!"

Angela, Peter, Cybèle, Bruce, a quartet no longer, and never again to be. Great Minds against Themselves Conspired. Who were they, and how and where?

The Angel

Let's begin with Angela, the wife. Wife she was, and known as such, Mrs. Angela Warden. But she herself cut no mean figure in the small community of Indian Springs. For one thing, her beauty shone out refulgent, even in the bleaching desert sun. Refulgent. It had become a favorite word for her husband. Peter.

"Shee with her beauty blazing," he often thought, singing to himself the canzonet they had sung together the night they first met at a music party in Berkeley. For each of them "Party!" had not meant beer and Roofies, but the gathering up of parts and instruments, and a evening of madrigals, string quartets, piano trios, and each New Year's Eve, a full performance of Carmina Burana.

The earworm circled and circled in Peter's brain,

"*Shee with her beauty blazing, Shee with her beauty blazing,*" over and over, without going on to the rest of the Elizabethan text, "*Which Death might have revived — him of his sight, and me of hart deprived.*"

But why go there, little earworm, when Peter's heart was *not* deprived? Angela Warden loved her husband passionately, deeply, and with all the understanding twenty-five years of marriage might bring to an educated, sensitive, mindful woman.

The opening of the canzonet, concerning blind Cupid, asks the question "*Doe you not know how Love lost first his seeing?*" And the answer? — "*Because with mee once gazing/ On those faire eyes where all powers have their beeing...*" Blinded by beauty, Peter was. And that was true for Angela too from the first moment he arrived, he with his tousled black hair, his fierce brows, and his great dark eyes shining on her, taking her in, his own beauty blazing beyond her belief.

That night, as well as singing, they played together the Mendelssohn D minor trio, she on violin, he on cello. Reader, if you don't know it, head quick for YouTube and take a listen. You'll learn a lot about the nature of Peter and Angela's meeting and marriage. The intense glow of the opening theme, pregnant, yearning, fierce, breaking out into the glorious lyricism of the second theme, arcing, roller-coastering, twining in aerial duet. Listen to it if you would know their song.

The string parts of the trio are relatively easy, just right for a first date, just right for an 18-year old violinist to hold her own against a 22-year old cellist. But the piano part is a bear. A grizzly. A towering Kodiak, standing on hind legs, nine-feet tall, charming in its way, but man, there are a lotta notes.

And taming the bear that night, even while sight-reading, was a young, I-can-play-anything pianist, attractive enough in a genius-musician way, a newcomer to the Berkeley scene named Bruce Fiedler Boynton, he of three names. Which was odd, given how embarrassed he was if thought related to Arthur Fiedler, conductor of the Boston Pops. His rant on "pops" concerts was worth hearing, but I'll spare you.

Angela married Peter after a season of dating and duetting. They appeared to have no children. We need not yet pry into why, but they seemed to have no children. And it was a good thing, too.

An Angelic Childhood

Angela Johansson was one of those golden California girls much celebrated in the freewheeling time, a stately, fine bird, with glorious blond hair, free-falling down her ballerina back, or else done up in complex Russian princess braids adorning her head, displaying her swan-long neck to great advantage.

A single child of a rich, Southern Californian family, she had had it all: private school, violin, ballet, voice lessons and French lessons, clothes from Rodeo Drive, and carefully selected beaux — at least until she went off to college at Berkeley, and parental surveillance willingly weakened.

Her father, Robert Johansson, AIA. had studied with the elderly Frank Lloyd Wright, and was one of the successful transformers of organic Prairie School style into that of desert modernism. The wealthy communities northeast of L.A., especially Palm Springs, had been his developmental playground, and he became famous — and rich — as word spread of his ingenious desert-architectural innovations.

Neither Robert nor Birgit, his Swedish wife, were disappointed when Angela chose to migrate to Berkeley. It was time for their treasure to breath some northern air, to take off on her own and demonstrate — to herself, and to the family circle — what such childhood enrichment might bring about. It was 1976, and much of the Sixties madness had tempered. There were not so many druggies on Telegraph Avenue, the chain link fence surrounding People's Park had already been torn down, and the property leased from the University by the Berkeley City Council. With donated labor and materials, the Berkeley community had rebuilt and managed the park in a close-to-normal manner. Robert himself had designed the playground equipment. Civilized, progressive, it was a fine place for their cherished daughter, far enough away for independence, and close enough to visit.

It was two weeks into her first semester that Angela noticed a three by five card on the music building bulletin board. PARTITA!, it said, and that's all, except for an address close to her dorm on Durant. She showed up after things had started, and found herself among faces familiar from the cafeteria, from the orchestra, and from her class on Philosophy of Literature. She spent this first PARTITA! sight-singing madrigals, and vowed to bring her violin thereafter. The norm seemed to be vocal-instrumental-vocal-instrumental throughout the night, and she'd rather participate than sit anything out. On her third evening, Peter walked in — as above.

The Warden

Peter Warden had grown up in and around Cornell University, where his father, Eliot, was an associate professor of music history. Being a Cornell brat meant growing up in an "enriched" educational environment, which involved being tolerated ("cute") at university activities as a mascot or pre-pre-peer. In his after-elementary school hours, he painted with the art students, and even saw nude models; he swam in the lap pool, did menial work in the greenhouses, poked around in the university library, and watched enthusiastic undergraduates torture rats.

When he was only two, his mother, Anna, had been killed in an accident driving home to Ithaca on a snow-blinded New York State Thruway segment south of Syracuse. The road had turned, but she had not. He was raised half-orphan, but with a large university surrogate family.

As a music department pet, he got to watch student rehearsals, and meet the world-class musicians who came through Ithaca. His most life-consequential afternoon involved a rehearsal of the Schubert Quintet by some famous quartet with a foreign name with its extra player, some famous Russian cellist. For the rest of his life, Peter would remember that day, when, already late at age 12, and having finally been allowed to draw a bow across Mister Rostropovich's Strad, he decided he must play the cello. What came out of that precious box frightened him by its depth. Frightened, but enticed.

Though John Hsu, faculty cellist, usually taught only advanced students, Eliot Warden asked his colleague about cello lessons for Peter. Hsu agreed, and even sold the Warden family an old student cello for a very low price, including a soft case and bow. It was no Strad, but even then, from day one, drawing the bow across open strings, young Peter felt the mysterious power of the machine he held between his legs.

A Cursed Childhood

But Peter's enriched childhood became even more enriched when, in May 1968, along with eight other clerical colleagues including his brother, Ted, Dan Berrigan chose to napalm several basketfuls of stolen records in the parking lot outside the Catonsville, Maryland Draft Board.

For the past two years Berrigan had been the director of an organization for all religious groups on campus, the pastor of the Cornell Catholic Community, and a friend to Eliot, the musicologist, helping him with liturgical music research. Neither he nor his son had been at Catonsville. Peter, certainly, had not even known about it. But unknown to both, that little protest would be a life-changing event.

In early October, the Catonsville Nine were tried in Federal Court, and found guilty of destruction of federal property, and interference with the Selective Service Act. They were sentenced, individually, according to their organizing roles, to one to three years of jail time, with fines totaling $22,000. Dan Berrigan was one of four who went underground rather than reporting for a three year incarceration. Of all of them, he was also the most annoying to J. Edgar Hoover, popping up here and there to give lectures and sermons, and then disappearing again. FBI hounds don't like being out-foxed.

"Going underground" meant living with different friends from one week to the next, and Eliot Warden was one of those friends, having co-taught a class with Father Dan on the history of ecclesiastical Chant. He lived with the Wardens for a short period in late summer, 1970, and was there apprehended by slow-witted gumshoes.

To them he said (and Eliot had this on tape): "My apology, good friends, for the fracture of good order, the burning of paper instead of children. How many must die before our voices are heard, how many must be tortured, dislocated, starved, maddened? When, at what point, will you say no to this war?" Peter Warden had kept and cherished that tape.

But Hoover was triumphantly incensed. Snatching Berrigan was not enough - his aiders and abettors had to be punished, too, and Eliot Warden had been caught in a flagrant *delicto*, sharing a meal, a table, and a roof with the offender. Hoover called the Tompkins County DA, and had Eliot arrested for "harboring a fugitive".

Conviction was easy. Here's the relevant text of the New York State law: S 205.50:

> *A person "renders criminal assistance" when, with intent to prevent, hinder or delay the discovery or apprehension of a person who he knows or believes has committed a crime or is being sought by law enforcement officials for the commission of a crime, he:*
> *— Harbors or conceals such person; or*
> *— Provides such person with money, transportation, weapon, disguise or other means*

of avoiding discovery or apprehension; or

— Prevents or obstructs, by means of force, intimidation or deception, anyone from performing an act which might aid in the discovery or apprehension of such person or in the lodging of a criminal charge against him.

Honest Eliot Warden, under cross-examination, admitted doing these things, lending Berrigan a bit of money, and "deceiving" the state police by not reporting that a fugitive from the law had asked to stay chez lui.

Berrigan was sent to federal prison in Danbury, CT, for eighteen months. To the jury, he had said,

"I have never been able to look upon myself as a criminal and I would feel that in a society in which sanity is publicly available I could go on with the kind of work which I have always done throughout my life. I never tried to hurt a person. I tried to do something symbolic with pieces of paper. We tend to overlook the crimes of our political and business leaders. We don't send to jail Presidents and their advisers and certain Congressmen and Senators who talk like bloodthirsty mass murderers. We concentrate obsessively and violently on people who are trying to say things very differently and operate in different ways."

They convicted him anyway. He was released in 1972.

Eliot Warden was sent for 24 months to the Attica Correctional Center, a maximum security state prison in Attica, NY, a three hour drive from Ithaca . He said nothing memorable to the police, to the jury, or to his family.

Prisoner 1593 was composing a song to the famous lines of Attica alumnus, class of '69, Willie the Actor Sutton, a text known to every student there:

Why did I rob banks?

Because I enjoyed it.

I loved it.

I was more alive when I was inside a bank, robbing it, than at any other time in my life.

To me the money was the chips, that's all.

Eliot Warden died there on September 13, 1971, a bullet through his heart. Peter was just eighteen. His enriched childhood had exploded.

Angela was shocked to hear all this.

There was more:

New York Governor Nelson Rockefeller had been attending a meeting in Washington when he was told about a prison rebellion at Attica. More than a thousand prisoners, mostly black, were holding 38 prison employees hostage. They were demanding (hard to believe these days) "safe transfer to a 'non-imperialist country'."

The governor would not come to hear their complaints of brutality. He never did visit the prison. After a five day standoff, on Sept. 13th, a helicopter dropped pepper gas into a crowded yard. During the melee that followed and six minutes of volleys from hundreds of guards, there were 29 inmates and 10 hostages dead, and 80 prisoners wounded, some fatally. Eliot Warden had been one of them.

The governor expressed his amazement that "not more had been killed." The medical examiner's report claiming that no atrocities had been committed by prisoners on hostages was dismissed, as the examiner was "a known leftist," and "the prisoners' demands transcended prison reform and had political implications."

What went on in the fog of war, and who shot Eliot Warden, no one would ever know. A surviving prisoner left this poem scrawled behind him. Peter had clipped the article quoting it, and carried it around in his wallet:

It was a day of terror, and everybody was sure;

That the events took place, they never witnessed before.

They deliberately murdered us, without a shield or any defense

By Ku Klux Klans disguised as troopers with little or no sense.

They made us crawl through the mud, like a snake crawls through grass;

And deliberately shot a few of us, because we didn't crawl too fast.

I heard a trooper yell, kill the niggers if they lift their heads,

Some shots rang out loudly and a few brothers were dead.

They made us take off our clothes and walk in an S-shaped line

And walk through glass, or get a bullet in your behind!

They told us to give up peacefully and we wouldn't get hurt.

And as we did what they told us, they shot us down in the dirt.

People think we're fools, to struggle and put up a fight.

But who are the fools but the people who refuse to fight for their human rights.

The things I don't understand now, time will make clear to me.

But what I do understand now, is that oppressed people must take a stand to be free.

So when you look back on September 13, and the year 1971, remember those who died in Attica without a prayer or a gun!

–Attica brother

Peter Warden, ex-music department brat, principal cellist of the Ithaca High School Orchestra, decided to study criminal justice in college. Because Cornell had no relevant course offerings, he enrolled at UC Berkeley, famous, even infamous, for its radical School of Criminology. It was 1974.

Two years later, his cello strapped to his back, he walked into a PARTITA! gathering attended by an attractive newbie. That night, he played a Mendelssohn trio with her. After that, they were an item.

The Pianist

L et us not forget that the success of the Mendelssohn that night, and thus the rest of this story, was carried largely on the moderately kyphotic back of the I-can-read-anything pianist with the thick, horn-rimmed glasses, he of the three names, Bruce Fiedler Boynton.

It was 8:35 in the morning of 9/25/58, time for a baby boy.

Marcia Agnell Boynton knew it would be a boy, because her friends had determined it three times in a row at three baby shower games, using three different methods — a pendulum, a deck of cards, and a ouija board. What's the probability of three independent tests all agreeing? 12.5%, her husband assured her.

Fred Boynton knew it would be a baby boy because first, he was quite certain it would likely be a baby, second because September 25 was the calculated due date and Marcia was always on time, and third, because September 25 marked the birthdays of

Glenn Gould, Shostakovich and William Faulkner —
and they were all boys. Two, Marcia remarked, even
played the piano.

A Curious Childhood

A quirky baby, he. All seemed normal until Marcia
noticed that the infant seemed more attracted to
objects in his field of vision than by her or Fred's
faces. Granted, they were not the most attractive couple, she too heavy, he too thin according to the charts,
but still they were "mama and dada", and one would
have thought that to have had some sway with little
Bruce. But no, he preferred studying his rattles and
stuffed animals, and later the geometry of his trucks
and blocks. "Empty Nest already," Fred joked. "He's
in his own dimension," Marcia glossed. The nursery
smelled of patchouli, *avant la lettre*. "It's calming,"
she opined.

There were some charming body movements. As
an newborn on his back, he would reach up with both
hands and wiggle his fingers. "As if playing Bach,"
thought Fred. And they resolved to have a piano in
the house, though neither really played.

On the other hand, there were some troubling body
movements. As an infant, Brucie had labored continu-

ally to prop himself up, contorting his body, and arching his back, the better to see the world. No crawling for him, but upright walking at ten months. "Gifted," they thought. As a toddler he babbled constantly, and was using full sentences by two. "A little adult."

A little adult with frequent tantrums, though, and lapses of his usual verbal skill when "being emotional". But he could be instantly calmed by giving him a complex object to study — a watch or a wrench or a clickable ball-point pen. Captivated, he ignored his tormenting parents, and entered his other world.

His first child psychologist explained it all as a need for pleasurable mastery and autonomy. Fred and Marcia had brought Brucie in for "willfulness".

Asperger's?, you are wondering. Somewhere on the low end of the autism spectrum? Fortunately, in the early 60s, not all child behavioral quirks were medicalized, and Dr. Spock's *Baby and Child Care* was on the way to becoming a bestseller second only to the Bible. Fred and Marcia eventually chilled out into a vague optimism concerning their odd little man. The used old upright they had bought remained unused, as Bruce mastered the details first of dinosaurdom, then of nautical knots, then of sports statistics, and later concerning the issues around JFK's assassination. He plotted the geometry of Book Depository to car, the proffered path of the magic bullet, and announced with great conviction that the official story was incredulous. He meant difficult to believe.

When Fred brought home a small Wollensak reel-to-reel, the engineering of magnetic recording captured young Bruce's imagination. His world now appeared as a presenter of sounds. He took the machine and its mike all over the house to experiment with the best method of recording doors opening and closing, dishes (a dish) breaking, the sound of roaches in the dark (none), his mother snoring, his father snoring, his parents snoring in duet, his own delivery of "Is this a dagger that I see before me?", and late but not least, the sound of the piano in its low, medium, and high registers. And also, reaching down inside, plucking, striking, and stroking metallic objects across the strings.

The trouble was he couldn't really play anything. He could hit the keys and play notes. When he held the right-hand foot pedal down and struck a note, the fading vibration fascinated him. But he couldn't make this putatively musical instrument make music. Which bothered him. Then really bothered him. Then bothered him immensely. He asked for piano lessons.

Fast forward, or ">>" as it said on the Wollensak,

to 1969, age 11. He had already fired his first teacher as "insufficient" and had been on his own independent-study curriculum for three years. He could already play all the two- and three-part inventions (by heart), and was halfway through the first volume of the *Well-Tempered Klavier*. He didn't practice all that much. A certain genius there.

Though he knew every baseball, football, and basketball statistic in all leagues back to the turn of the century, he didn't play sports. When Fred tried to teach him to catch, he would turn his back and let the ball hit him. Afraid of his hands getting hurt, Fred supposed. He was a lefty with an IQ of 172, and therefore without many friends. In high school, actually, no friends. "I'm too old for this kind of thing," he said.

Brainy Bruce at 17 was an accomplished musician and a budding intellectual, more interested in math and music than in hanging out, socially awkward except with others sharing exactly his style and interests, introverted, efficient, and serious. He was also a bit of a mouth-breather, somewhat stooped, gawky, seeing the world through thick glasses. Not a big catch for the girls. Nor were they much of a distraction for him.

With one exception. Looking somewhat like a

human being in his usual duds, he found himself at one of his first PARTITA gatherings accompanying a young soprano in the fifth of Hindemith's *Songs from the Life of Mary*. He didn't know much about Mary, and barely understood the German text — something about Joseph being suspicious — but for the rest of his life — as if seeing the event focused in a telescope across space and time — Bruce recalled her blue velvet dress, with long brown hair flowing over it like a wave. And he was suddenly filled, in some indescribable way, with the longing to actually be a girl. At the moment, and in the wildness of Berkeley in the seventies, this did not seem entirely impossible. But it was transient, more a groping in the darkness against some warm and pleasant resistance. At the end of the song, Joseph lifted his cap to the departing angel and sang praise.

Bruce, too, at a PARTITA? For the author's convenience?

No, it was because Marcia had been hired as a new age nutritionist in Food Services, while Fred had snagged a safety manager's position at UCB. They were able to make their escape from Urbana, Illinois, hoping for better weather and a place where, his parents being university employees, Bruce would be able to attend a good school for free. He started PARTITA!-ing as a senior in high school, and by his freshman year at

Cal, he was an off-campus pianistic fixture.

On campus, he was a math major. Why? One, he was good at it, as many musicians are. Two, his parents, with whom he was still living, thought it might actually get him a job. But most important, most driving of all, was that he liked — loved — vectors, those little arrows with direction and magnitude. The whole world was made of vectors, vectors coming at you, vectors shooting from you, vector arrows and spears and crossbeams and nets, aggressive, defensive, mushy and hard, Debussy and Webern vectors, Wagnerian mycelia vectors embracing, strangling, suffocating one lifeworld and squeezing out another. And beyond Euclidian, vectors axial and gradient, waving and Poynting, P-vectors, null vectors, spin vectors, four-vectors. Vectors. He loved 'em. That's why he could play or memorize anything.

But vectors or no, he was harassed by dolts in the non-music/non-math community, ridiculed for his peculiar looks, pimpled with permanent adolescence, for his R. Crumb gait, his thousand-mile, coke-bottle stare, and the stains of pork buns and chili-dogs down the front of whatever sweatshirt he was wearing. Arguing from Newton's Third Law, the Law of Cause and Effect, along with the Law of Inertia plus the Laws of Macro- and Microcosm, all finessed with the Law of Vibration, he figured he should join the Air Force ROTC. He might get hassled by profane, sadistic drill sergeants, but at least, they'd have to call him "Sir." AFROTC. Not because he had an afro, but because he was a Luftmensch.

Rotsy students at Berkeley were about as welcome as Muslims at Yom Kippur, but since he was often the target of contemptuous vectors anyway, why not flaunt it in uniform? He might acquire the non-mathematical virtues of courage, loyalty, and esprit de corps, the better to armor himself (though perhaps at the cost of diminished compassion) against the slings and arrows of Telegraph Ave.

His instructors in Aviation and Military Science respected him, though he affected the irritating habit of addressing his teachers in the archaic military third person: "Would the Major like me to further explain my thinking?" Further explanation was usually not wanted.

He did not shine in Field Training or Leadership Lab. He graduated a commissioned officer, and after graduation, he disappeared from view.

The Singular Wedding Of
Peter And Angela

You'll never guess who the officiant was. Franz Schubert. Yes, that one, all the way from Vienna. It was 1978: anything could still happen.

QUESTION AUTHORITY was not just a bumpersticker, and the authority most questioned was anything with a badge, anything thus labeling itself as questionable. Red Brigade freedom fighters abducted and killed Aldo Moro, the prime minister of Italy. Socialists in Afghanistan, though few in America had ever heard of Afghanistan, overthrew the president and signed a treaty with Moscow. Even the Shah of Iran caught the bug: in June, he had had the Chief of the Savak Secret Police arrested on charges of torturing prisoners. The President of North Yemen was killed by a bomb. In August, left-wing Sandanistas seized the National Palace in Managua, Nicaragua (What a wonderful town!) in an attempt to depose Anastasio Somoza. And in Berkeley, besides fighting

Proposition 13, Peter Warden and Angela Johansson decided their marriage was no business of the state — or the church.

On a glorious Saturday in November, Peter and Angela were married at a regular PARTITA! evening. None of the other singers and players suspected what was happening.

Her clothing that night was not out of the ordinary, but like much of female fashion at the time, it was imbued with sufficient magic to transform, without changing a ribbon or a bead, into a magical garment, as the occasion demanded. As she took her violin out of its case, every fold of her skirt, every tuck on her blouse, was lurking with power, enveloping her in a glow more than nuptial. Peter and Bruce were dressed normally, if slightly spiffier than usual.

The three sat down to read the exquisite slow movement of the Schubert B♭ trio.

Bruce, mischievously smiling, lay down two measures of a gently rocking lullaby, and Peter entered, pianissimo, in a high register, playing a melody to melt the heart. With a little flourish, having grown to forte, he sank down again to accompany Angela's statement, their two lines caressing one another far more intimately than physical bodies could approximate. Bruce added his version in gentle octaves, smiling all the while, as the couple licked around the melody with playful, insistent tongues. The tune would flirt with minor keys, but briefly enough to simply affirm its compassionate sunshine.

The middle section is stormier, forced by the piano on the others, but with the kind of exertion which only strengthens the singing pair above it. Nevertheless, as her part relaxed to let the piano lead, Angela felt a passing strangeness she had never before experienced. This, she knew, was her wedding ceremony, yet here and now, of all places, she felt unfaithful to her groom. As she was transported by the music, she imagined he couldn't understand as well as she the greatness of what moved her, or what was truly going on. All colors, all faces, her very bow and strings had been enhanced by the moment, and no, she was not on drugs, she was riding on Schubert, the curves of his melodies and their gorgeous modulations. In some unutterable way, everything seemed different, loftier, expanded. She felt free, and strangely free from Peter, his cello, and his designs on her, attractive as they were. He — and all else — seemed to be on the other side of some membranous veil. A little longer, and she might have slipped out of her own being, beyond reach, a space of inviolate solitude, an emptiness of boundless truth.

But the A section returned, and she was called again to be in charge, the one responsible for pivoting on a long C, crescendo-decrescendo, to bring back the opening theme a tone higher, and for inviting Peter to come join her in these more daringly harmonized regions. Back to earth she dipped and rose, but with a complex seed planted within her, as if by some holy ghost.

Schubert had taken the three through his ten minute conjugal sermon, and it was time for the "I do"s, the public pledging of allegiance not to country, but to spouse. They had chosen their moments. Angela's was in the third measure from the end, using her little sixteenth note figure to articulate "Yes, yes, I do," singing the pitches in her beautiful voice, and emphasizing her commitment with a long, accented B♭.

Peter chose the next occurrence of that figure to offer his "And I do, too," singing it in harmony with Angela above, and while it was Angela again who nailed it down with another long, accented B♭ an octave higher than her first, Peter repeated the phrase in duet with his cello, and then with his cello alone. There was a short silence in the world, and then the couple played their affirmation figures together, to bring the service to a close on a long-held fermata. And they were both astounded.

Only Bruce noted that their final instrumental statements, their affirmation figures, were in contrary motion, hers climbing to a high E♭, his descending to an E♭ four octaves below it. Bruce's notes spanned the inner space between, and he wondered what all that distance meant. But then, as scripted and assigned, he channeled the ministering angel, and in his best mock-Austrian-fat-man-with-little-spectacles accent, said "Hiermit erkläre ich Sie zu Mann und Frau."

And then he added, unscripted, unexpected, "And may that glory which rests on all who love, rest upon you, and bless you, and fill you with happiness and a gracious spirit...and despite all changes of time and fortune, may all that is noble and lovely and true abound in your hearts, and abide with you, and give you strength in all your days together. Amen." I don't know where he got that text from, I don't know if mathematicians are capable of composing such a text. All I know is that he said it, and perhaps we have now detected something somewhat cryptic about him.

Everyone else in the room eventually realized what had come to pass. It did take a moment for the Ellefson apartment, somewhere on Durant St., Berkeley, California, USA, Planet Earth to re-establish, and then there were tears and applause and hugs and deep breaths and backslaps when it did. Bruce then announced, "For income tax purposes, Angela will be taking Peter's last name." There was politically correct laughter, but that, in fact, was the case.

Difficult Rehearsals

I mentioned that the three musicians had sat down to "read" the Schubert slow movement. I lied. While PARTITA! norms generally involved sight-reading — music grabbed impulsively from the Cal or Berkeley Libraries — this performance, given its momentous mission, had been scrupulously rehearsed in the basement of Morrison Hall, the UCB music building.

Funny thing: even though rehearsals were for a wedding, the thing the trio did most was fight. Or rather, Peter fought with Bruce over approach, style, phrasing, meaning, interpretation. Though Angela had taken some convincing about the anomic ceremony, by the time they were in rehearsal, the basics of the event were agreed upon. What was at issue was classical vs. romantic anomie.

Peter was the Romantic. Given the unique situation, he wanted to break traditional performance rules. You know, "Let us break their bonds asunder, and cast away their yokes from us." Like that. Bruce, on the other hand, thought the music could certainly

break its own bonds without any help from undergraduate musicians, especially those whose future
lives were at stake as a result of the performance.

For every start there was a stop, and for every
stop, a re-start. How loud, how soft, how fast, how
slow, how phrased, how accented — with this piece,
it seemed there was nothing Peter and Bruce could
agree on. Angela, though annoyed by all the men-like
haggling, was content to simply play it as she felt it,
and as first (and only) violinist, to bend the piece in
her direction, without all the bickering and abstract
debate. Plus, Bruce had the annoying habit of calling rehearsal letters by clever, smart-ass names, as in
"Take it from M, for mnemonic," or "Back to G for
gnomic," or "Let's go from P for pterodactyl, or from
R for articulation." It got old fast.

Yet there was something in this struggle we had
better keep in mind concerning romanticism and the
breaking of bonds.

The Desert Waits

Why is it that the Sun Belt, in spite of drought, remains the fastest growing region of America? Are Americans so overstuffed, so from-supersized-soda edematous they feel a need to desiccate? Has the American night become so black, its politics so dark-sided, the only recourse is to seek the sun, equipped with Ray-Bans?

Who is winning in the current race between flood and desert? Overall, the answer is clear. The desert awaits.

It took Mr. and Mrs. Peter Warden three decades to answer its call, turbulent years of many wars, inter-personal, cultural and international, and after 9/11, global, and intentionally endless. The desert seemed physically, spiritually, a place of escape, a last refuge for silence and reflection. Balzac thought that "the desert is where God is, and man is not," and if so, what better place to settle, to flee the crowd and seek for self? Awash in scarcity, what better place to learn what is sufficient?

The Mojave is such a place, a hot dry desert two-thirds in California, but reaching eastward into southern Nevada, western Arizona, and the far southwest corner of Utah. If you love creosote bushes, yucca, and the occasional Joshua tree, the Mojave is for you.

Peter did not love any of these, but a lucrative job offer from the Nevada Department of Corrections was too good to turn down.

You will recall that in 1974, Peter, armed and burdened with his dead father's tale, had enrolled at Berkeley with his eye on the pioneering School of Criminology. But before he could begin his junior year, in that 200th anniversary of the land of the free, the University administration, feeling threatened by a decade of student and community uprisings, closed the school down to protect the University from "too many" radical ideas. But not before Peter had taken the two courses which set his mind to pursue a career in prison administration.

A look at the contents of the (in)famous Crim.100A and 100B will tell us a lot about Peter's ethical interior, and the intellectual environment in which it was formed.

100A discussed the definition of crime, ideology, and the current theory and practice of crime, including the crimes of imperialism, capitalism, racism, sexism, and crimes by the state and its servants, such as the university. While "liberals" in the discipline limited criminological study to the crimes of the powerless, and their technocratic or social engineering solutions, the radical faculty at Berkeley taught that "criminals" were actually victims of larger systemic crimes which denied whole classes of peoples and countries their full human potential and right to survival, self-determination, and dignity.

No feather in the cap of the University Board of Regents, a group of gentlemen appointed by the governor, consisting primarily of lawyers, politicians and businessmen who have commonly donated large sums of money to certain election campaigns planned to "sanitize" the university.

But Peter had taken Crim.100B, which examined social control and the criminal justice system. The class studied the Progressive Era in which the modern Criminal Justice System and the Welfare State was constructed, the race and class struggles of the period, "Americanization", and the rise of "rational" models of social control. They looked at juvenile courts and reformatories, sentencing, the eugenics movement, the rise of private police forces and their counter-insurgency techniques imported from current military incursions, the rise of social control agencies and their relationship to the political economy, liberation struggles international and domestic, the current injustices of the criminal "justice" system, and the "hegemonic functions of social control." Peter was enraged and inspired. You can imagine how this went over in Sacramento.

The administration pressured faculty to let go untenured, "too radical" professors, and to deny tenure to those too threatening. And in 1976, at the end of Peter's sophomore year, the School of Criminology was shut down.

But not before Peter had already imbibed the Marxist concept of praxis — the combination of thinking and actually doing — and had contributed many hours working for community control of the police through Berkeley elections, helping Berkeley High School students oppose federally funded police-in-the-schools programs, and lobbying against the proposed Center for the Study and Reduction of Violence at UCLA, a laboratory for psychosurgery and behavior modification experiments on prisoners. His notion was to make criminology serve the oppressed rather than furthering their control. His perspective was based on an understanding of human rights and social liberation, and not on property rights of the privileged, a view which threatened the

very interests the University was created to serve —
those of Capital.

In the spirit of official '76, his program was abolished. But in the spirit of another '76 his worldview became established. The subsequent decades were filled with the kind of anonymous, long-haired, backstage organizing which is the life of any political academician. Having graduated summa cum laude, BK, with honors in Sociology, he pursued an MS in Justice Studies - Public Administration, and had been hired as faculty for periods long enough for him to be denied tenure at several California State Colleges, and the University of Oregon Portland School of Law. His wife — and his cello — accompanied his travels.

Angela Warden (neé Johansson) impressed at every job location. She majored in violin performance, and blew away a music critic of the SF Chronicle with her senior recital evening entitled "B+B...+B". The Chronicle did not usually cover undergraduate recitals, but word had gotten around about the extraordinary nature of this one. The Bach Sonata #3, with its astounding solo fugue movement, the rhapsodic, energetic solo suite by Ernst Bloch, and to end with the biggest bang, the fiery, difficult Bartok Sonata for Solo Violin — with its hair-raising fugue — demonstrated the great range and depth of her technique and spirit, and had the audience peeing in its pants. Minutes of standing applause, in a day when standing applause was granted only to the truly extraordinary. Among other superlatives, the Chronicle called it "death-defying".

While Angela was practicing Bartok, other Berkeley students had organized a campus women's center, and in 1976, a year before her graduation, the school responded to student pressure by initiating a Women's Studies Program. But it was the shattering Ms. Magazine story on battered women, the smashed face on its cover, that turned Angela's attention to things less musical, more related to the interests and activities of her husband.

Her coveted "sub" position with the San Francisco Symphony gave her the time — along with 20,000 other women from around the country — to attend the National Women's Conference in Houston — the first since the historic Seneca Falls Convention in 1848. It was her father who financed the trip. It was her husband who encouraged her to go. She took her violin, and a heavy mute, so as not to lose a day of practice.

But she practiced not a note. Her days were filled with heated debate sessions concerning the ERA, reproductive rights, childcare funding, sexual orientation, the rights of minority and aging women, and above all domestic violence. In the evening, instead of retiring with her violin, she went out with new friends from the "No More Cages" group to plan anti-violence organizing. While separate, and for the first time physically apart, she had never felt closer to Peter and his work. She was happy their birth control seemed to be effective.

For several decades, through sundry moves and many orchestras, she, unlike any of her musical colleagues, mixed a life of high-level practice and performance with a passionate engagement in feminist struggle and social change. And given Peter's work and political milieu, she managed to escape the bourgeois tendencies of second-wave feminism. Her interests, her clients, were women among the poor, the battered, the imprisoned. In each of their locales, she either helped found, or joined in staffing a women's rape crisis center. She carried a beeper — turned off during concerts — for emergencies and late night calls, and each successive Warden apartment included a spare room for all too-frequent fugitives.

Peter and Angela often wondered why they alone among their musical friends pursued such political activities, and why their "classical" music was seen as irrelevant, even counter-revolutionary, by their political colleagues.

When, in December 2002, *The Nation* sent a special double-issue entitled "The Power of Music" to their Portland home, they opened it with anticipatory trepidation. Would the magazine's lefty scan be blind, as usual, to the revolutionary message of "classical" music? Would the highly educated, morally aware, philosophically sophisticated, politically savvy editors and writers supply their readers with any reflection on a millennium of radical musical expression? Would the self-censorship and cultural/political omissions Peter and Angela expected from mainstream media be duplicated here, *mutatis mutandis,* and the double-issue be filled with obvious suspects and current celebrities? Their suspicions were, alas, well-founded.

They didn't get it. They continued not to get it. In "classical" music — from the tenth through the twentieth century — the west had inherited a cornucopia of profundities prompting and announcing social change at every step along the way, educating human consciousness towards ever-greater complexity of perception and thought, exploring unarticulated emotional and spiritual depths. The great composers had always demanded and developed in their listeners, their "fans", precisely those sensibilities humans need to confront the most difficult issues they face — structure, otherness, variation, modulation, time, change, form, dissipation...love.

Angela thought of the room in which the Eroica was first performed — its aristocratic, gold-leafed curlicues, its elaborately carved chairs. She thought of Beethoven's assessment of the "princely rabble" that would seat their asses on those chairs, and the shattering indictment with which he would assault them in the name of freedom. *Seid umschlungen, Millionen,* he demanded in the Ninth, masses embracing in the kiss of the entire world. "Tell it to George Bush and the IMF," Peter remarked. He and she discussed Bach's intensity and structural investigations, Brahms's deep sensuality, Mahler's catalogue of stylistic fusions, Wagner's engorging instability, Bartok's *mesto* variations in the Sixth Quartet, Stravinsky's primordial landscapes in the *Rite*, Berg's evocation of interstitial states — they could go on and on, and in and in. Were all these irrelevant to the left, and to its goals of head and heart?

And the means of production? Though there were surely classical stars and consumers, by far the greatest number of sounds were made by amateurs at choral or orchestral or chamber music rehearsals and performances, or playing at home — a democratic, participatory picture of growth, education, and community, growing since the eighteenth century.

Yes, the rock art and artists in the music double-issue

spoke strongly to America and its times. But they were not the only music relevant to the left.

Peter wrote a letter to the editor urging recovery of the western musical heritage, and the key role political/cultural journals like *The Nation* could play if they so chose. The letter was never published.

Domestic violence continued. Guard unions pushed hard for prison expansion. Private prison contracts demanded occupied beds.

And all the while, the desert was waiting.

THE HIGH DESERT

Yes, the high desert. 2,000 feet or more above sea level. A land of pastel shades and enormous stillness. As they got out of the rented car for Peter's interview, the sound of their feet on Mojave gravel was all that was to be heard, that, and the cry of a distant bird, and the faint vibration of a jet painting a vapor trail out of Las Vegas.

Nevada's High Desert State Prison was the largest and newest in the state. There were plans for what was to become a large southern Nevada prison complex. What would that mean? Peter would see.

The prison opened as the millennium turned, in more than a million and a half square feet of space.

In 2009, new construction was completed to add an additional 1344 beds for what was by then 4,000 prisoners. And with that addition came the need for more staff.

It was 2009. Peter was taken on as an Associate Warden in charge of Programs. Serving the wardens were ten lieutenants and thirteen sergeants, 400 security and 67 support staff.

It was most unusual for Wardens to be appointed via their academic credentials. They usually came up through the ranks, most beginning as correctional officers, COs, i.e. prison guards. And prison guards had to be tough. Smart, yes, but with street cred and alley smarts for the yards, the catwalks, and the cells.

Peter could play tough, but that wasn't the Peter that played Brahms. It was a fortuitous combination of circumstances — his having seen the ad in the *Journal of the American Correctional Association*, of HDSP clicking in his mind as one of OJ Simpson's stays, of his and Angela's becoming slowly weary of Portlandia — and from the other end, of a shift in public opinion: prisons increasingly stood for big-government waste, and high-paid prison guards looked more and more like welfare queens and greedy public school teachers. To fend off the Nevada legislature, and to maintain an expansionary income in the midst of the great recession, the NDOC needed to boast "something new", some first in American corrections. Peter Warden, academic heavyweight but with only cello callouses on his hands, was that something — a handsome token-intellectual fit for sub-leadership in a program which could pay lip-service to modern correctional thought. Personal and Educational Programs for Prisoners. And you should see his wife!

To better give the reader an idea of Peter's zone of operations, the author can do no better than to quote part of an official document:

High Desert is designed to meet the department's operational philosophy to ensure a safe secure environment for the community, staff responsible for inmate management, and for the inmates assigned to the facility.

The High Desert State Prison will be the most secure prison in the department. All cell doors in the units are operated by rack and pinion mechanisms from the unit control rooms. The prison has five (5) perimeter towers and one (1) yard tower as well as interior gunposts above the housing units, operations center, culinary building, and in each dining room. In addition, the complex has a lethal electric fence, perimeter observation towers, and a "no-man's land" inside the fence allows officers in towers to observe any inappropriate inmate movement toward the fence from inside the facility. Each two (2) housing units together form a secure compound and can be operated in whatever manner may become necessary. Access to the main compound is controlled by an armed officer in a protection post above each two (2) units.

Sounds homey.

INDIAN SPRINGS

A new era for Peter and Angela, a new landscape, with new challenges. The postal address for the prison, and the closest town, was Indian Springs, NV, population 991 — before their arrival.

Used to moving from job to job, they packed up efficiently and drove a medium-sized U-Haul of books, music and household goods out to Lincoln Lane in Indian Springs, where a house trailer just south of Route 95 awaited them on its one acre of land. Two small trees in the front yard attested to the small, deep water table which allowed Indian Springs to sport some green against the surrounding desert. The tacky wood paneling throughout, and the wall-to-wall carpeting in the dining room and bedroom reminded them warmly of their grad school beginnings, and of the future blessing of moving out and moving on…

…to the desert dream house Robert Johansson was designing for his daughter, her husband, their future children, himself as architect, and himself and Birgit to visit now that he had retired. Designing homes for rich clients had had its drawbacks, since they seem to feel they could tell him what they wanted, and he had always to lower his sights to their amateur imaginations. Now — especially since he and Birgit would be paying for it — he could go hog-wild designing the ultimate desert home for the kids to live in. Harmonized with its surroundings, using its tans, light greens and burnt siennas, minimizing the difference between inside and out, cool and warm as needed, "in retirement", he would finally make a name beyond his already-made name with this dwelling — his Bavinger House, his Leff Residence, his Falling Water.

Location, location, location — a challenge out there with carceral and military neighbors. But one would enter this house and feel free in the deepest way a house could create. In dry conditions, dry, dry, dry, his grandchildren's home would have shade and water, perhaps a pool, even if he had to join hydrogen and oxygen himself by methods devious and quixotic.

Driving southwest on Cold Creek Road past the prison gave little hope until the land began to rise and fall unpredictably. On the way to its end eighteen miles on, and a thousand feet higher, the vegetation grew denser — from creosote and rabbit brush to Joshua trees and, after a dozen miles, pines and piñons, cottonwood, willow, scrub oak, sage, prickly pear cactus. And wildflowers, purple, yellow, red. At the termination town of Cold Creek, a developer's paradise beginning to stir, with a real creek, cold too, three ponds, wild horses, and views of the snow-capped Spring Mountains. Cool, fresh water.

Too easy for Robert to build up there, not enough problems to solve, too much mixing with the familiar upper class and the regulatory criminals that serve it. The desert would be his sand-ocean, the site his Pequod, and the landscape subjugation would be his vanquished Moby Dick. For Peter and Angela, a few miles back toward the prison and Route 95 was a few miles less to commute, and a few miles closer to town. They were sure Robert would find them an optimal spot.

The story of that siting became part of the family history. Robert figured the water up at Cold Creek must go downhill to somewhere, and he might find it further back on Cold Creek Road in more heroic territory. What was his dowsing rod? A single Joshua tree on a small, lone hillock. "The Joshua" old Mormons called it, somewhat garbling Exodus 17:11, conflating Joshua's and Moses' upraised arms in triumphant battle against the Amalekeits.

The Joshua's arms present a more complex picture. Stiff, ungraceful, savage and weird, Yucca *brevifolia jaegeriana* is a treelike structure of spines constructed to prevent most animals from climbing from below. This isolated specimen was twenty feet tall, twisted, brash, silhouetted against a reddening sky. "This must be the place!" Robert shouted, or something like it, misquoting Joseph Smith, who never shouted it or anything like it. Would Robert had known the real invocation, Sharlot Hall's 1911description of Joshua, the Yucca Palm, with its "serried scourges" born high:

Stern penance do you for old wrongs
Mayhap, or saintship seek from pain;
With suppliant hands that never win
The benison of cooling rain.

Enough literary scholarship. The fact is that Robert yelled something enthusiastic and this-must-be-the-place-ish upon spying the tree and the spot.

The Joshua was right. It *was* the place, and uniquely so. Drilling down 435 feet (and who but Robert Johansson would be so convinced as to do it?), McKinney & Sons,

50

drilling and boring contracters from Las Vegas, hit water. Twelve gallons/minute, not very fast, not very much, but clear and cold, and enough to support the famous-to-be Warden House, Cold Creek Rd., Indian Springs, Nevada. The McKinney hydrologist thought it must be a rare small storage cavern, a fault in the rocks below.

For a celebration of place, Peter opened a cardboard box he had carried from home to home for almost a quarter century, and unveiled the cherry-wood urn holding Eliot Warden's ashes. That beloved man who once walked the earth, taught his students, and played his clarinet, was whirled away by the wind until the ash became wind, the wind ash, and the desert swallowed up that ash we all are made of.

During zoning shenanigans, purchase, planning, foundation work in shifting sands, building, and furnishing, the temporary Warden residence was still in the trailer on Lincoln Lane in Indian Springs. But the new land had been marked.

Water, water…There *is* no shortage of water in the desert, just the right amount, the perfect ratio of water to rock and sand, an optimal distribution which allows generous spacing among plants and animals. There is no lack of water — unless you try to build a city where no city should be.

A Message from Sekhmet

Weekdays, Peter went off "to prison" at seven, after a quick cup of coffee. Angela had much of the day to practice (for what, for what?), play desert tourist, and shop for one dinner at a time at the RiteAid in town. It was there on the bulletin board she saw the handbill that would transpose her life into a new key. On green copy paper she read

Sekhmet Temple of Goddess Spirituality
Cactus Springs
THE GODDESS WELCOMES YOU

Cactus Springs, she knew from her map study, was the next (small) dot on the map along Route 95 — a town, a village, a few houses? — northwest of Indian Springs. For temporary housing, she and Peter had restricted their search to south and east of town. But it wasn't that far, and this sounded worth investigating, at least for amusement's sake.

Angela turned south off Frontage Rd onto Goddess Temple Rd. — an actual, official, State of Nevada road sign — where did they make these things, in Peter's prison? Must have given the prisoners a good laugh, or did the signs emerge from the women's pod? Goddess Temple Rd.

A few miles down the one-laner, a hand-lettered sign pointing off to a small parking area "Park Her", it read. Whether "Her" was a typo, or referred to the car, or to herself, or to the location orthographically gendered — was unclear. The functional ambiguity embraced all. From the car, a three minute walk on a high-desert landscape trail to something indicated as "THE TEMPLE ⇨".

And there it was up ahead, a white structure not quite a building, certainly not a temple, but more like a large upturned white cup or narrow bowl, with large arches open to the weather in its four sides, four ceramic turrets at its rounded corners, and topped with a larger open dome of overlapping copper hoops, if not a temple, at least a recognizable shrine.

Posted on a signpost outside was a parchment under glass which seemed worth stopping for:

A Message From Sekhmet

Welcome to the Goddess Temple of Sekhmet. I am so happy you have come to visit me. I am the Goddess of fertility, the desert, and much more. Fire is my element, and the Sun is my messenger.

Visit with me, show me your love and sincerity. I also want to know of your dedication to purifying this Earth and honoring every spirit. Can you welcome death and know its true intention? What does rage and anger satisfy?

Angela thought of the Air Force Base, three miles distant, and of the Test Site or atomic weapons lab or whatever they do half an hour away, and even of what must be going on at Peter's prison.

I do not want to conquer nor rule. I have given you the arts, mathematics, and sciences, to fulfill your needs, to grow and enjoy. Yet you are not satisfied without power. Why is power better than what is natural and abundant around you and the beautiful gifts that flourish in your garden?

Why do the nations, she thought, so furiously rage together? And why do the people imagine a vain thing? She hadn't played years of *Messiahs* for nothing.

It is not fear that I support, but a desire to wash your eyes, cleanse your ears and clear your throat. For then, you will see the smile, hear the birds, and talk the truth. When you understand this, then, there will be no bloodshed upon the earth.

[Channeled from Sekhmet to Patricia Pearlman,

Program notes for what is to come? she wondered. Desert feminist peaceniks? She breathed a touch faster.

Inside the shrine she found a central fire-pit, and four walls punctuated by the open arches, each wall dedicated to a different goddess. A short circumferential stroll introduced her to the Madre del Mundo, the Virgin of Guadalupe, Kwan Yin, the Goddess of Compassion and Mercy, many other goddess statues in niches and shelves built into the walls, and, at four feet tall, the largest icon of all, the black and mysterious Sekhmet herself, seated on a throne, surrounded by flowers, feathers, and crystals left by visitors, and fronted with a large singing bowl, its mallet waiting. The smell of freshly burned incense hovered in the air.

Sekhmet, with her lion's head and human body, seemed the inverse of the sphinx, but for Angela, was equally riddlesome and sphinx-like. Perhaps the bowl before her would speak in her voice, or yield some answer, or at least present the question.

Angela picked up the stick, set the bowl-bell lightly ringing by rubbing the leather mallet around its rim, developing a hugely-embracing D which filled the chapel space and penetrated deep inside her childless womb. With no further stroking, the sound lasted a timeless several minutes before the overtones disappeared beyond the walls, and up through the skeletal dome. She stood, transfixed, impaled.

In the extreme silence, Angela became aware of another presence, turned, and saw a shortish, red-haired woman of about fifty, standing in the southern archway.

"Hi. Blessed be. I didn't mean to interrupt, but I saw a car in the parking lot, and heard the bowl. I thought you might want some information, or a little tour of the grounds. I'm Candace Page, the resident priestess."

To Angela, she looked more like a small-town Republican city councilor than a feminist priestess. "I'm Angela Warden," she said, trying hard to focus in on quotidian reality. They shook hands. "Can you tell me something about the lion-woman here?" she asked.

"She is a very ancient goddess, with many names in many cultures."

"But why a lion, here? Lions, for one thing...kill."

"Sekhmet is many things, potential violence, yes, but she is beautiful, sensitive, amorous, playful — and like all powers, both creator and destroyer, gardener and weeder of the garden. One story I love is how, when she was outraged at human evil, intending to devour humanity, she was tricked into drinking a large glass of beer disguised as human blood — probably by some corporate flack with a bottle of food coloring. Anyway, she got very mellow, and humankind was left to survive. So to speak."

"So you're saying..."

"Think about it. How we are drugged into giving up our power, hypnotized into allowing political and ecological destruction to proceed. An important lesson she teaches."

"But you'd have to know that story..."

"Not if you take in her image, her expression. And remember what the bowl said to you..."

Shaken by a forced re-entry from the world of the gong to an almost badgering political discourse, Angela parried with "I'd love to see the rest of the grounds, if you have time to show me."

They left via the north arch, and headed through mesquite and sweet-smelling creosote toward a stand of large cottonwood trees.

"I'm surprised to see all the greenery."

"The springs of Cactus Springs," Candace said. "This little island attracts lots of birds and animals — and the people who come to stay with us."

"Who are they?" Angela wanted to know.

"Oh, peace groups, women's groups, Shoshone, people like yourself, some who need a place to calm down or recharge. The test site out there is a hot spot for radiation, but this is a hot spot for positive feminine energy. There's our labyrinth over there, and to the right — those colorful benches are a social area. There's a cactus garden back there, a sleeping platform, and we're working on a rose garden."

"Who is 'we'?"

"Mostly me, but we do get volunteers, and when groups come through, they usually do a lot of work. I can always use more help. Interested?"

"I..."

"I understand. First visit, and goddess knows where you're from, though you've got Nevada plates."

"We just moved here. My husband works at the prison."

"Ah, the wonderful prison, new and shiny and high-tech."

"You know about it?"

"The Desert Experience holds vigils there. We've done several "wailings", too. We name the things we mourn about and moan and scream like banshees."

"They must love that."

"The prisoners do. They make fun of us, imitate us, jump around like monkeys, but we fascinate them, if only because we're women. We do it at the test site, too, and at the Air Force base, but we can't get as close, and the warrior-types who do see us have stiffer upper lips or something. We like the prisoners best. Here's the guest house."

They climbed two steps, and Candace opened the door to what might once have been a double-wide trailer with additions, but was now covered with the same white stucco as the Temple.

"We can sleep ten or twelve comfortably, as they come. Groups can make reservations. No charge. We hold lots of rituals. There's one tomorrow — new moon, women only."

"Men are allowed at other times?"

"We welcome everyone. All we ask is respect for Temple values: goddess spirituality, the gift economy and peace. No weapons, no alcohol, no violence."

Inside the guest house, beautifully furnished with feminist art, were a living room, a fully equipped kitchen, two bathrooms, and four large, labeled bedrooms — a Mother Room, a Crone Room, a Maiden Room, and most elaborate of all, Womb Room, curtained, kept dark, and lit in red, presumably for young women, mothers, the elderly, and... fetuses? Angela asked.

"No. Pregnant women, joyous or concerned. They come to better decisions after a few days here."

Thinking back to Berkeley and Portland, Angela asked, "Do you ever have domestic violence victims or women who were raped?"

"Often enough. Too often. But we have no support staff except myself, and though any of the women who visit could be helpful, people come and go, so I hesitate to really…." She gestured "you know" with her hands.

"I see."

Angela left that day thinking two things: one, that she would like to work up the tricky Bach Chaconne in the Temple, and two, that Indian Springs, and Cold Canyon could probably use a Women's Crisis Center.

Ach, Bach!

Thank God for John Calvin. Like Peter and Angela, Bach in his early thirties was still looking for a well-paying gig, and found one at Cöthen, as Kapellmeister to the twenty-something Prince Leopold, himself a talented harpsichordist and string player — at twice his previous pay. Life at the court was unceremonious and easy-going, and the young Kapellmeister with the burgeoning family became the prince's royal bud, devoting all his time to composition and playing.

The only hitch was that Leopold and his court were Calvinist, and no music was allowed in his plainly decorated chapel other than congregational hymn singing. So Bach had to stow his greatest compositional ambitions — his weekly religious cantatas, and giant works for organ — and concentrate on secular forms. Lucky for musicians! Out of Cöthen flowed a stream of chamber music, sonatas, concertos, and keyboard works. Sweet are the uses of austerity.

The six sonatas and partitas for solo violin, like the six solo suites for cello (which Peter adored and endlessly practiced), form the kernel of any string player's repertoire, the sweet spot blending soul and technical demand. The towering Chaconne of the second violin partita looms over any movement in any of these, inexplicable in its gigantic presence, a tail so wagging its dog as to entirely transform any concept of dogness. Joshua Bell once played it busking in the L'Enfant Plaza metro station for a story in the *Washington Post*.

Angela would perfect it here, master its finger-breaking double and triple stops, build her endurance to get through it. She imagined its epic chordal opening might resonate with the Temple's challenge to the weapons sites, its hymn-like middle section with the goddess's energy invoked and gathered, and its final section, wild, fierce and convinced, with the lion head of the goddess herself, before succumbing to the fatal glass of beer.

And practice she did, the God-like piece in the sacred space, yang to its yin, resounding. Angela became a familiar figure around the Temple, practicing Monday through Thursday mornings when visitors would be least likely, greeting the occasional interruption with long-necked grace, her beauty, as always, blazing. Her "I was just leaving" gave the visitors the space they needed to be with the goddess.

But she and Peter also began attending the monthly rituals, full moon the both, and she the new moon, and often she was asked to play, and did — slow and lyrical movements from the Sonatas and Partitas which seemed to fit the mood prevailing. At Beltane, she dared her first public performance of the Chaconne, standing high on the Sky Bed platform as thirty Wiccans danced around a bonfire below, slowly, quickly, even jumping through the fire as the music called them to.

About the notes rising in convection to the Mayday sky: Brahms had written to Clara: "On one stave, for a small instrument, the man writes a whole world of the deepest thoughts and most powerful feelings. If I imagined that I could have created, even conceived the piece, I am certain that the excess of excitement and earth-shattering experience would have driven me out of my mind."

All the Sekhmet participants felt the same. In case they had forgotten, they were that night indelibly reminded of why they bothered to live.

The Boss

Strange. Though Clayton Straud, the warden at High Desert State Prison, had worked his way up the correctional system ladder, from Correctional Officer to Lieutenant, to Assistant Warden, and now to Warden, he was actually a liberal. Liberal, at least, for the state of Nevada — or he would never have considered hiring Peter, a lefty from the People's Republic of Berkeley, Ph.D, or no Ph.D. He'd voted for Bill Clinton, George Bush, and Barak Obama. He'd known Harry Reid in the late sixties, when they had both worked for the United States Capitol Police, policing the same demonstrations. He was impressed with Martin Luther King, and his ability to draw a crowd which didn't need crowd control.

And what *is* a Nevada liberal, especially a Nevada liberal bureaucrat? Someone who believes in collective responsibility for the welfare of all — which in his case, meant voting higher taxes for state corrections. He liked Peter, though he knew he was a gamble, and he liked him most for his ability to impress legislators about the tax-saving potential for the tax-spending costs of his programs.

Peter liked his boss as well. He attended his addresses to civic orgs and fraternal orders. Clay's Assistant Warden for Programs played wing-man with impromptu backups to win support for Clay's reforms and his own experimental programs — and then could settle comfortably down to the eternal stony peas, frozen mashed potatoes, and fried chicken or boiled ham.

They both believed — Clay from his long experience, and Peter from his classes, books and heart — that prisons are not for punishment. Confinement was punishment enough, and the state's job was to make that confinement as comfortable and constructive as possible.

As part of his job interview, the warden walked Peter through the impressive physical plant. Opened at the turn of the millennium, and with newer units only one or two years old, the paint was fresh, the smell was clean, the barbed wire shiny, and the mountains were clear in the background.

They started in the visitor's lobby, and screened public waiting room. Then on to contact visitation and non-contact visitation booths. Peter got the standard spiel:

"This is the most secure prison in Nevada. There are 12 housing units designed to house 336 inmates each. Each of units 1-8 are separated into four (4) sections called "pods". Each set of two "pods" shares a common control center and staff office. Each set of two pods also shares a sally port and an activity room."

Peter loved the term "sally port", the controlled entryway between gates locked fore and aft. In his mind, he heard Angela singing, *"It was down by the Sally Gardens my love and I did meet."*

They walked past a hearing room with a one-way glass wall, an intake processing area, a master control room in each unit with observation, supervision, and unit control and inmate corridor control observation modules. Wherever they walked, their suits were greeted with careful eyes. "Morning, Warden."

"Morning, Swift, Morning, Montez." Straud seemed to know many names.

The ear worm sang, *"She bade me take love easy, as the leaves grow on the tree..."*

Each housing unit had a not-unpleasant dayroom, and an education area classroom. Four newer units circled a common athletic field with three basketball and one tennis court.

"The Clark County School District provides the

education program using 8 classrooms and 2 libraries. If you're hired, you'll be working alongside them,
and our own psych department."

"*But I, being young and foolish, with her would
not agree.*"

Across the yard were a gymnasium with a mezza-
nine, and a central dining room with fixed stainless
steel tables and cooking area. Peter toured the services
control station with its 100% observation, supervision, and control of loading and unloading areas.
Overall, he thought, an immense aggregate creature
of walls and bars and rooms filled with men shaped
and molded to its needs. Peter wanted to shape them
to their own.

We Never Know What We Are Walking Into

Prison reviews. Prisons get reviewed? Like plays and books and concerts? Seek and ye shall find.

High desert is worse than poor. The COs retaliate against any inmate who speaks out against mistreatment. What happened to free speech? The food portions are too small — like child-size — which is probably just as well because the food is horrible. Anyone who complains is thrown in the hole as an example, or just to keep you quiet. Yell at the walls. I know, I know — the inmates are here (usually, but not always) because they did bad things, but they're in to pay for their crimes, not to get tormented by the COs. What happened to rehabilitation? When they get out, they'll be worse than when they went in. If the top brass finds out about this stuff, there's always "an investigation", and then stuff gets swept under the rug and disappears. If you have a friend or loved one in High Desert, listen to what they say, and if your complaints are ignored, then call the central Corrections office in Carson City. And call higher up, call the governor. Things need to be changed at this place, desperately.

    Rayleen J, N. Las Vegas

This place is the worst in the state, and probably in surrounding states. It's just a training camp for CO gorillas. Watch out. Tell your loved ones to be careful and keep their hands down. It's the only way to survive. Good luck to you all.

    Gloria P., Tonopah

Just so you know, especially if your a first-timer, it can be very tough, very tense here. The gards are not really friendly, but also they are not complete assholes. It's like a front cause they have to keep order. But here are some tips.

    — Don't wear anything blue, even if its just a blue patten in your shirt, or they won't let you in.

    — Don't bring more than $30 — IN QUARTERS ONLY — and only in a clear plastic purse so you can buy food and drinks from the machines for you and your loved one. You can't bring in handbags or

*purses or wallets, but you can store your stuff in a
locker when you come in.*

*— You have to get on line and fill out the infor-
mation for who you are going to see. MAKE SURE
YOU HAVE THEIR ID #. Then you get checked in
and go through double doors and wait in line again
to be called to go through the metal detectors, and
get pated down like at the airport if you've ever been
there. You have to take off your shoes, and the floor
is ALWAYS cold and of course they have no carpets,
and then you have to go back to the metal detector
section again and give your ID to the guard at the
window. You get it back when you return. If you get
ok'd you exit outside to the next building where you
have to check in again and tell them who you want
to see. They'll tell you what table they will be at (as
if you don't recognize them after coming all the way
to see them) and then you sign in again. Then you sit
down to talk. No touching, or the guard will make
you leave. You can get up to buy drinks or snacks or
go to the bathroom, but the inmate can get up only
twice — once to go to the bathroom, and once to
throw out the trash. You have to be the one to chase
the kids. You should probly bring the whole $30 if
you have it, since everything in the machines is over
$1.50, and stuff adds up quick.*

SECURITY

Early in Peter's tenure, Clay invited him to witness a particular officer doing what he liked best — orienting the new fish just coming in off the bus. The two men in suits and ties stood behind one-way glass, looking into a room with twenty-five men still in street clothes, some old, but mostly young, some brown, some black, but mostly white, a dentist's nightmare of missing teeth, an ink-pusher's dream of meat wanting yet another tattoo. This is what came over the speaker:

"My name is Murillo, Lieutenant Frank Murillo. That's Murillo with a Y, not with Ls. Get it? Lemme hear you say it. Lieutenant MuriYo."

They said it with a reluctant participation in choral speech.

"I'm head of security, and you don't want to see much of me, I promise. You can call me Lieutenant

Murillo, got it? You are convicts. You don't have names unless I choose to learn them. Right now, you are just numbers. Carry your photo ID cards with you at all times, or you face disciplinary action — which could include the SHU. Anyone not know what the SHU is?"

A hand timidly raised.

"*No hablas inglés*, moron? The SHU is the Security…Housing…Unit. Solitary, to you. Six by ten. You won't like it for more than an hour I promise.

"Now as I was saying — We each have our jobs in this game. You are the convicts. Your job here is to lie, cheat, and steal from each other and from us, to snag illegal drugs, to get amateur tats, to sell drugs, make shanks, to fuck and suck each other like good little boys do. And our job is to catch you.

"This is a fancy, new prison. But you are not fancy, new prisoners. Just the same old shit. So I have news from the prison medical director, Dr. Bettman. You are statistically likely to have a combined HIV and Hep C infection rate of 60%. Now this is America and we have freedom of choice. So if you choose to use drugs here — and you will — remember, that's part of your job — then snort them, smoke them or swallow them. I would advise you not to shoot them. Dig?

"And Gentlemen, especially those of you who are more Ladies than gentlemen — if you have to get some cock action — that's part of your job — let your new friend suck your dick, not fuck your asshole. If you bend that way, there are plenty of fairies here hoping you'll find them. That's what freedom is for. America. If you stick your dick into an HIV hole, you're gonna get AIDS. I promise you. And if you get AIDS, you got nothing coming from the state. Our infirmary is chock full of dying faggots and fairies."

Some scornful sniggering toward fairyland.

"Some of you geniuses no doubt think getting a tat is ok if you hand Joe Michaelangelo a new needle wiped on your sleeve. Well, think again. Every day we confiscate tat guns from deep up someone's hole, coating itself in shitbugs, just waiting for you. You stand warned.

"And by the way, don't get caught. Doing anything. On our pay, we don't need more work, and we might get angry if we have to deal with you. And above all, stay out of my way, or you'll be sorry.

Now, what's my name?"

"Lieutenant MuriYo," most said. It's possible that someone actually grumbled "Asshole" or "Fucking Asshole."

"What's that? Who said that? No one said that?

OK, then, *you* said it." Murillo pointed at a greasy 18-year old with a ponytail and goatee."

"I din't say nothin…"

"That means you didn't say my name when I asked you. Just as bad. Take him away, throw him in the SHU, and bury the key."

A CO, on cue, grabbed his arm and walked him away down a corridor.

"As I said, *señores*, don't get in my way. *Hasta la vista*. See you when I see you."

And he walked out of the day room.

Quite a performance.

"What did you think?" Clay asked, as they walked back to offices beyond the gates.

"Is that for real? Is that what he's really like?"

"Good eye, Pete. It's only an act. He thinks playing the cartoon bull will help the men bond with one another against him, the asshole. He thinks it's good for prison peace for distinctions to be sharply defined. Your job, our job, you low, me high. The clearer the class separation, the less interaction, the less chance for friction."

"Yeah, I've heard that one before. It's called apartheid."

"He knows that. But in some way, he really believes it. And it's been effective: we've had no big trouble here in the ten years of our existence."

"Well, that's your doing, I'd say," Peter offered his boss.

"Thanks. Yes, to some degree. But I get to play good cop to his bad cop."

"It's a system."

"Right. But, you are now — whether you realize it or not — mucking it up as far as Murillo is concerned."

"How so?"

"Oh…fraternizing with the enemy. Being just one of the guys. Some days not wearing a jacket and tie."

"It's 105 out in the yard."

"Yeah, well…Murillo's into dress codes. It's the code part, not the dress, he's concerned with. Prison work is a haven for people content with any stable status quo. They are seriously threatened by mavericks on the staff, anyone trying to change the system. The staff don't want change and the inmates don't want change. Neither does Frank. You've got to be careful around him. He's on your case since you took Angela on tour, and had her watch a drama workshop."

"He's got the hots for my wife?"

"No, maybe, I don't know. But he thinks the men — not your workshop guys, others — got a little too jumpy." He handed Peter a scribbled-on sheet of notepaper:

"Que galla!"

"I wouldn't mind pullin on that mama's tittie."

"That's one fine, scandalous bitch."

"Jaina, hombre, jaina gloriosa!"

"Man, old Warden, what a guy, stickin his peter into that!"

"Chichi, chichi!"

"Who wrote this?"

"Dunno. A Mr. Fly. Possibly named Frank."

Peter nodded.

"OK, no more Angela at the prison."

"Play nice with him, OK? As they say at Rotary, 'When the cup is full, carry it even.'"

Disturbing thoughts on the bike ride home. Peter had often noticed how attractive Angela was to other men — how could she not be? But he'd never been jealous, only proud of her beauty blazing. Not proud of himself for having caught her. He didn't even "catch" her. They came together as naturally as violin and cello, linked and twisted not by ego, but by the lovely music they made together. When he visualized them "as a couple", he saw two handsome people, well-matched, a ten with a ten, or at least a nine (he) with a ten (she) — but that image, medium shot, reflected a deeper beauty in their relationship, two individuals spending their days separately perhaps, but ever keeping faith with one another, and in the higher calling they served together, a calling often expressed by, but not limited to their music.

And yet somehow, odd as it may seem, the ragged, pencilled notepaper burned in the shirt pocket over his heart, this miscellaneous collection of admiring commentary not from potentially seducing beaux, but from men out of Angela's class entirely, light years, men who, if they ever even got near her, could never win her heart, or her mind, or her soul, and who, if they ever got near her body, could never merge with it but could at best, only rape. "At best" and "rape". Those words uncomfortable together, even in a sentence. Yet why only now was he disturbed? And why did that irritation hold a faint jealous tinge?

He had had no siblings that might have buried seeds for psychoanalysts to water. He had a father, yes, but as a father-figure, Eliot was hardly a Laius to be slain, and his mother had given herself to him as much as a boy-child could want. More. Too much, even. Did he feel some way inadequate, a man needing to be replaced? Self-esteem had never been an issue before. Was he himself, unconsciously feeling a need to "wander", projecting it on the men? Hell no. By the time he parked the bike, he was ready to toss the note in the trash, and he did.

He didn't tell Angela what had happened that day. Stroud had recommended that he discuss with her the unlikely possibility of one or the other being taken hostage during a mass break, but he didn't want to alarm her. And he didn't want to sully the kitchen table with news of Frank's note. It just seemed best to keep it inside.

ON PRISON PROGRAMS
Murillo

Warden Warden, it will soon become clear to you that nothing works. Nothing. None of your programs. You'll see. They'll come and they'll go, and new ones will show up in correctional journals but...

Peter

That's simplistic — "nothing works." You assume offenders are incapable of learning new behaviors.

Murillo

Correct.

Peter

It's self-serving. What are you afraid of? Less recidivism, fewer criminals, fewer jobs? We always talk about the men avoiding responsibility for their behavior, but the fact is that "nothing works" encourages *us* to avoid responsibility. The men are untreatable, so we can't be held responsible for their improvement or deterioration.

Murillo

You know, I dropped in on Arithmetic Class last Tuesday. Fractions — you'd think they were trying to learn set theory — whatever that is.

Peter

For them, it *is* set theory. Just as hard, and they don't see the point of it.

Murillo

No kidding. Those colored and Mexican boys don't give a damn about fractions except when it comes to cutting up an ounce of stuff. The only reason they enroll in these classes is to impress the parole board. Get your asses in school, learn to read and write and do fractions, and we'll think about cutting your time.

Peter

I know that. The men have their reasons, and we
have ours.

Murillo

Who's we, hombre?   And even if they do learn
something by accident, they're still not going to read
anything except ads and street signs. They're already
expert on speedometers. Don't you find it depressing?

Cage The Rage

Anger Management had been the first new program
Peter initiated. Six twice-a-week sessions. "Cage the
Rage" he called it, hoping to appeal. He and the staff
psychiatrist facilitated. At the first meeting, everyone went around the circle introducing themselves.
Nothing in particular required, just tell what you'd
like others in the group to know about you.

Most responses were taciturn and leaden. Except for
one. When his turn came, one Craig Nelson, #3957, 33
years old, second admission for armed robbery, had
this to say:

"I've always been a straight-up con. I don't give a
fuck what you guys think, Doc Gall and Doc Warden.
The judge sent me here to do my time, and that's all

I'm going to do for you. I'm here cause parole may let me out earlier if I come and complete. I'm not here to play your games. Yeah, Number 3957 belongs to the State of Nevada, but I am telling you clear, I am here to do my time, not to be rehabilitated by your stupid-ass fucking programs. And I'm not going to do what you want me to unless I feel like.

"When I get out there again I can make up for all the shit going on here now. I'll be free to live the way I want, and do what I want. I can shoot dope and rob and rape and steal. I can live fast and good as I want, and when you nail me again, I can come back for a vacation and wait it out till next time with three hots and a cot all paid. And I'll know I can always get out again, and again, and again. So dig me — I do the time this time and next time, no prob, no big deal. The judge thought he was going to teach me something with his sentence, but he doesn't get that I'll be free to dance on his grave. And maybe on yours. Just so you know. Fuck you very much."

"And you, too," thought Peter.

"Inmate code," though Dr. Gall.

Wiping Up The OJ Spill

It seemed thematic, yet an unexpected modulation,

for their dinner conversation to turn to discord over a recalcitrant prisoner. Granted, that prisoner was OJ Simpson, for Peter a killer who had beaten a murder 1 rap via fame and money, the American way. But the Warden table that night was as divided as America — and Angela was on the black, the prisoner side, of the board.

OJ had been a guest, but only a guest, the previous year, when he spent a few evaluation weeks at HDSP before being sent off to Lovelock for numerous Nevada felonies, including armed robbery and kidnapping.

"He was a giant in the black community," Angela insisted, an old-style hero in the age of gangstas and DJs and rappers. 'The Juice'. He was health-giving OJ for them."

"And for you?" Peter asked, unusually wary. Her reaction seemed to him overly complex. She admitted believing him guilty, but thought his crime, so detailed in the media, and so thirstily followed by the public, must somehow belong to a more general American pathology, especially concerning women."

"So? Doesn't that make it worse? Do you think he should have been acquitted?" Peter asked, incredulous.

"No. But I think the verdict, its reception by blacks, has to be understood as part of their larger under-standing of the great crime of American violence. Like a Bosch painting. For them, he's not guilty, not individually guilty. It's kind of fascinating."

"You're fascinated, not repulsed?"

"Well yes, sort of. Both."

"Is it because he's so handsome?"

She gave him a look he had not seen before, and he apologized.

What with their days spent apart in different worlds, both were aware of a growing, and unaccustomed distance between them. Not miles. Feet, maybe. Inches. Distance nevertheless. It was Angela who addressed it first:

"Peter, let's work on something hard together. It'll be good for us."

"You think we need therapy?" he joked.

"Nooooh, don't be silly. Here's what. I'm itching to work up the Ravel duet." Peter knocked back his head and rolled his eyes.

In his Sonata for Violin and Cello, Ravel attempts to evoke an entire symphony with one compositional hand tied behind his back, and his free hand restricted to two fingers, albeit index and thumb. While almost every one of his works requires instrumental deftness and high technique, and his players have to learn, as Nietzsche said, "to dance in chains" in order to play him, the final result is often a tour de force of sonic richness. In the duet, the chains are the insufficiency of single lines, the harmonic poverty of the two note chords, the lack of melodic accompaniment. This was the kind of game Ravel liked to play.

His solution, and the challenge to the players: the astounding mobility of the two parts which have to manage being everywhere at once, in a serpentine play of counterpoint, difficult to track, circling ostinatos, collaborative and conflicting, each pursuing and losing, losing and pursuing the other, diabolic pizzicatos on some huge metainstrument, violin and cello the same and not the same, finally roiling itself apart, expanding and desperately popping its own balloon.

"What's the matter?" Peter asked. "You need a day job?"

The notes are hard enough to play, but the piece is harder. Where is it going at any moment, where are the phrases, what is it saying, is it dialogue or competing soliloquies, or two instruments ignoring one another, and in what arrangement?

But they stuck with it, and were ready to try it out on others at some appropriate occasion. Only ten minutes long, they had put four months into working it up. Their baby.

HOUSEWARMING

The obvious moment was at the house warming, the presentation of chez Warden and its crew to their new friends and community.

Who was to be invited and expected? Robert and Birgit Johansson, of course, along with several ex-colleagues from the firm, and Martin Filler, architecture critic from the *New Yorker*, along with John Dixon, editor of *Progressive Architecture*, both of whom promised reviews. Clay Stroud was there, and the three other assistant wardens from the prison. Peter considered inviting Murillo, but thought better of it, feeling the modernist opulence of the house (courtesy of his father-in-law) might seed class issues beyond the political and philosophical ones between them. And Candace Page, the priestess from Sekhmet, who brought a lovely small statue of Hestia, virgin goddess of hearth, home and family. Henry and Frances

Perkey came, with a box of party edibles from their store, the one and only Indian Springs Market and Emporium.

It was June. Angela had posted an OPEN HOUSE ALL WELCOME sign on the Perky's bulletin board — the very cork on which she had been first notified of Sekhmet, and right next to the Temple's latest welcome, more professional now through word processing. Though she and Peter did not expect many strangers, they felt prepared for any who might come.

But never did they expect this one.

* * * * * * * * * * * * * * * * * *

TRIGGER WARNING
In his 1964 movie *Dr. Strangelove or: How I Learned to Stop Worrying and Love the Bomb*, Stanley Kubrick uses the song "We'll Meet Again, Don't Know Where, Don't Know When" to accompany the final montage of world-destroying explosions.

* * * * * * * * * * * * * * * * * *

There was something familiar about him. The bulging eyes behind thick glasses, the large, loose lips around a mouth-breathing mouth, the tall, semi-kyphotic frame, and then the distinctively irritating voice:

"Hello. I trust you remember me." The immaculate clothing, the military bling, could not hold their own against:

"Bruce Fiedler Boynton!"

"Captain Bruce Fiedler Boynton, please. You may call me 'Captain", or for old times sake "Capt."

"Bruce!"

"Capt."

"What are you doing here?"

"What are *you* doing here?"

They could not fail to meet again, of course, since the three fed on the same energies. And today, when they did meet again, as though by pure coincidence, or by the author's plot, it was as if they coalesced, and could almost no longer be without one another. Berkeley, Nevada. Almost.

"No, really, what are you doing here? It's been, what, thirty years...

"Twenty-nine. And this is Indian Springs, Nevada, crossroads of the world, or crossroad of our worlds at any rate. How should I *not* be here?"

"Peter's working at the prison," Angela said.

"And I'm protecting your lives, fighting for freedom and democracy in foreign lands."

"And I'm a crisis counselor at the Sekhmet Temple."

"Ah, Sekhmet, those Furies who occasionally

harass us at the gates with their anti-musical banshee chants and wailings. I'd rather take in a consort of drones.

"Seriously, what are you doing out here?"

"Creech, of course. I'm Captain of Mathematical Cyberspace, working on counter-counter-cyber intelligence. At the moment I've taken leave from the routine weekend of I and I — Intercourse and Intoxication."

Peter and Angela stared openmouthed in disbelief.

"You work at the base?"

"Head of a small elite group of government hackers, charged with "offensive cyber operations" and groundbreaking capabilities to defeat adversarial cryptographic efforts. How to stop them from stopping us stopping them. My particular project is to prevent the breaking of drone encryption. You can sleep well tonight, as long as one of our Predators doesn't crash into your new house."

"Oh, come on," Angela objected. "You're allowed to talk about this stuff, your work?"

"Angela, my dear, what have I told you? Is it not public knowledge that Creech runs drones, and that electronic codes require encryption? If I didn't exist, they'd have to invent me."

"Are you still playing music?"

"If you can call it that, on an old upright in the canteen late at night. The Bad-Tempered Klavier. You string players wouldn't want to hear it, though Charlie Ives might love it. Are you?"

"In about half an hour, you'll see. Can you say Ravel Sonata?" Peter asked.

"I can say it, but can you play it?"

"We'll see," Angela said.

Like a true musician, Bruce hung out at the food table, snagging cheeses and cocktail franks, pocketing non-melting cookies for later, and talking to no one, but observing, observing.

When the time seemed right, Peter clinked a spoon upon a sonorous glass, and announced,

"Friends and family old and new, from near and far, Angela and I welcome you to our new home, designed and built by that guy there, Robert Johansson — who also helped design and build my lovely wife."

Applause. A blushing Angela.

"We thought you might want to listen in on what Angela and I have been pecking at for the last few months.

And so they pecked, not without some mistakes, but with the effect the Ravel duet usually makes: unspeakable astonishment.

The party went well, with no untoward incidents, and the three agreed to meet the following weekend to discuss getting the old trio together again in this unlikely venue.

The first problem, of course, is that pianists need pianos, not bad-tempered claviers. Especially for the demanding trio music they'd be playing. It turned out there were quite a few piano dealers in Las Vegas — who would have guessed? Should they go window shopping? Craig's list offered the usual mix of who-knows and junkers. Probably not the best way to shop for a soulmate.

The two most obviously prior questions were 1. how much could they spend, and 2. where would it go? The second was easy — clearly in Peter and Angela's living room, which had light, space, and necessary quiet. The Creech canteen ran a far-distant second. But where in Peter and Angela's living room? This question reached out toward number 1. A high-qual-ity, "concert" upright might play and sound all right, but it would have to be up against a wall, no?, and thus the arrangement of players might not be optimal, especially if they branched out from trios. And besides, there *were* no walls. There were thermal windows on three sides with exquisite desert light, and the fourth side consisted of an "entertainment center" squared, bookshelves and equipment artistically arranged for practicality and effect. If a concert upright was chosen, it would have to stand somewhere in the middle of the room, its rear bare as with a hospital johnny, looking like nothing so much as a Kubrick monolith with teeth.

On the other hand, concert grands ran $30 thousand and up, $40K for a Steinway or Bösendorfer, and the civil servant/volunteer/airforce captain group had nothing like that kind of money to spend.

There were "baby grands" for under $10K, some for even half that. But Bruce squashed the idea in its cradle. A baby grand, with its tinny-sounding bass strings of insufficient length, were for bourgeois wannabes, looking for furniture, not sound, he proclaimed.

Preconceptions aside, they would head to the big city next mutually free time, and Bruce could bang on as many, and as many kinds, as he liked till he found something acceptable. They decided they could each put in $3K. If that didn't do it, Angela might consider asking her still-indulgent parents for the rest. Bruce would gather a team of UAV grunts to move it in a military vehicle. If he were challenged, he'd chalk it up to health club activities.

The cherry on the whipped cream on the body of the shop would be a visit to the Liberace Museum Bruce had heard about. He wanted to play — or try to play before being arrested — on Chopin's Pleyel piano in the fab star's collection.

When their guests had left, Peter and Angela walked from their flagstone veranda out into the desert twilight, their distended shadows reaching out far overland. Notwithstanding occasional traffic on 95, it was quiet. More than quiet. Desert quiet. Quiet with the desert's dearth of insects. An immense stillness.

As they walked away from the house the sound of their feet on the desert gravel and the rustlings of tiny night animals drifted into bottomless silence. The empty expanse absorbed all resonance, wrapping every sound in self-enclosure, flatly soft and private. An oval, descending sun hung and trembled – then slowly fell, mellowing the red light over the sand, diluting the distance to the mountains on the west, as a wind high above cleared a fuss of thunderheads to the south, washing the air and bringing forth a scent of sage.

Those mountains, those strange rounded hills, parched, naked, rising isolated, concise, contained, yet major characters on Peter and Angela's new horizon, barely changing shape as winds slowly wrap them in their own shards and sweepings. Gazing at their silhouettes at night, hiking them by day, the couple could not penetrate all the secrets they hoarded. Guarding them in silence, tiny lizard Fafners, patient armored plants, stones protecting sunbaked rocks, all children of blinding heat, aridity, the spawn of emptiness.

The evening sky had become a giant rainbow, and then a blazing orange half-dome backlighting a sparse sea of indestructible creosote bushes, straggling, tough, brown life-forms, waist-high to a man, standing dark now before them, the local version of vegetable beauty. Above, a ghostly jetliner from Las Vegas traced a silent, red, dissipating line up the sky. A dry, night-desert chill spread under a rising gibbous moon. The air grew cold.

"Hard to imagine the city out here," Peter whispered, nodding up at the plane.

"I think about it all the time," Angela demurred. "It's archetypal, that space-age thing tensing against this ancient earth right here."

"It's sad," Peter said, "that thing up there…"

"And those things at the air force base," Angela added.

"Yeah. Especially those.. sad that those things are what all evolution has come to. And the most horrible thing is that this, here…" Peter gestured at the quickly darkening space around them…"This is exactly what spawns it. Creech, the prison, they don't see all this as romantic or even beautiful. It's just big. It's empty. Hard for prisoners to escape. The air is clear, so the military can afford to pollute it without violating air standards. Always good flying weather, clear sky 300 days a year."

"As I said," Angela continued, "archetypal. Yin yielding yang, yang bearing yin. Beethoven's rough sublime."

"I suppose. But I can do without the jets and the drones."

"They can also do without you," Angela observed. Her intent was not clear, but Peter preferred to let the topic drop, and bathe once again in the silence, going gentle into the dying of the light. He put his arm around her shoulder to warm her in the sudden cold.

Twilight was past, and the desert night began its first movement, its exposition of the gleaming, dreaming stars. Time was no more, and all was space. They returned, silent, hand in hand, to the house.

Tortoise

The ambient temperature within Robert Johansson's celebrated Desert House was constant and comfortable, day and night, all year round — the result of many structural and equipment variations — like the angled fly floating above the house — and a ton of California architect money. You can't take it with you.

While temperatures in the Mojave can vary by as much as 80° in a single day, temperatures in a desert tortoise will vary by quite a bit less. And for far less money. That's because desert tortoises spend 98% of their time in their insulated burrows under relatively constant humidity. One Mojave burrow was found to harbor 20 of them.

They don't have to come out a lot because they eat most of their food in the spring, when they chow down on succulent succulents. As in Robert Johansson's Desert House, they employ very clever, efficient means of storing water. They don't pee, for instance, but store urine in an enormous bladder, and as summer approaches and the plants dry out, they draw water from that cistern of urine. Like the astronauts do. And since the desiccated urine then grows dark and viscous, their shells and scaly skin limit surface evaporation to almost nothing. Desert tortoises pass their summers at an osmotic concentration which would be fatal to most animals — like the Wardens.

It's a shame that the maneuvers of off-road and military vehicles affect them the way windshields affect bugs. Not only do vehicles destroy ground crust, burrows and forage, but tortoises have been found beheaded, and some flattened in military carrier tracks that seemed to have swerved to hit them. People have mentioned baby tortoises being great skeet targets. One prison guard from HDSP boasted of lining up dozens of hatchlings for a shotgun execution. Another placed ten under a wooden plank, and drove along it. Yet desert tortoises persist. Millennia of training in hunger, thirst, and exposure. Tortoise abstinence and endurance.

As they approached the house, Peter and Angela saw one.

Buying A Piano Is Not A Simple Task

Las Vegas provides the best demonstration of the permanent impermanence of man in the desert — largely because its invincible presence is everywhere. Wherever humans have not built, wherever concrete is not poured, the desert abides — even in the pedestrian islands in the middle of the Strip. Humanity seems a mere experiment in alien territory.

Buying a piano in the desert is not a simple task. Especially when one — before all else — must see the Liberace Museum for fear that it might close early.

Liberace's taste ran to bejeweled, red, white and blue

Rolls Royces, a 24-carat gold-plated 1931 Cadillac, a collection of 42 pianos, including — in addition to Chopin's Pleyel and George Gershwin's Chickering — a mirrored concert grand which takes nine men and a fork lift to move, a white llama fur coat with a 16 foot train, a diamond ring with a stone the size of a lemon, and stage outfits of mink and feathers worth three quarters of a million each. Liberace was once the highest paid entertainer in the world.

The Museum's visitors are silent and reverential — almost as though they're at the Sistine Chapel or the Vietnam memorial. They read and take notes on the information in jewelry display cases and posted near pianos and cars. Mr. Showmanship also had flair in pedagogy and museumology.

But his taste in museum siting did leave something to be desired. The famous Liberace Museum shares a small shopping center 2 miles off the Vegas Strip with Tatiana's Hair Salon, a storefront Asamblea Apostolica, an Aladdin Market, and a refrigerator magnet store. A Seven-Eleven and The Pinball Hall of Fame lie across the street.

Being one story, the museum is not quite an imposing structure. Nevertheless, it tries hard, encompassing two contiguous storefronts, one for cars and pianos, the other for clothing and jewels. Atop its entrance flies a giant pink neon piano floating on an undulating keyboard and topped by Liberace's florid pink signature. To its right, a large wall — three overlapping pages of childish music in 2/4 — nudged by a giant portrait of the child-man himself. You can't miss it — and you easily can.

But the Captain's GPS nailed it right quick, and its digital voice assistant called the turns correctly, all the way down 95 and through the heart of town, evading traffic on the problematical Strip. Not that Bruce didn't want to try his smarts at the blackjack table, but the string-players reminded him they had piano-buying to do.

Bruce's target, the Chopin-played late eighteenth century Pleyel, was set off behind a velour catenary supported by two ornate brass stanchions. To a civilian it clearly meant "Do Not Touch". To Captain Boynton, it meant "I can probably reach it if I lean way over." Although a catenary curve superficially resembles a parabola, Bruce was versed enough in these matters to know that it actually traced a hyperbolic cosine function. And given that catenary curves are used in suspension bridges, plus the fact that he was sort of hyperbolic himself, the Captain, having ascertained the coast was clear, decided to support himself with his left hand in the middle of the curve, and reach out with his right to the keyboard. The center, as Yeats predicted, did not hold, and the stanchions collapsed inward, sending Bruce sprawling forward enough to shove the piano bench into the pedal assembly, toppling the candelabra standing left of the music stand, said candelabra smashing on the keys ringing out a chord neither Chopin nor Pleyel had ever imagined, and the guards came running.

Bruce, ever creative, quickly gathered his rumpled self up off the floor and announced his intention to sue the museum for slippery floors. The tables preemptively turned, the guards, then the museum director made nice-nice, made sure he wasn't hurt, and refunded the price of his ticket ($15). The trio left early, Bruce's desire having been thwarted. He was not interested in llama skin coats.

Over the course of the afternoon, the trio visited four piano dealers. The Captain sat in each showroom, and tried the recommended pianos which their collective pockets would tolerate. At each instrument, Bruce played two or three minutes of the same four selections, his choice explained in the car on the way down: the Scarlatti G major sonata would be for delicacy and fluency, the Bach C#minor fugue for sustained gravitas, the Hammerklavier fugue for wackiness and unplayability, and the Brahms A major

Intermezzo, just to be nice to the other customers.

At 4:30, after fifteen or sixteen mini-concerts, Bruce called it a day without making a decision.

"You know," he remarked, driving home, "trying out potential pianos is a lot like dating from the personals. You study and consider the specs, but then you have to go out to dinner for a first date. Not that I would know, never having been on a first date or any date."

Peter and Angela wondered silently if this were hyperbole or literally true. After all, who would go out with him? And what woman (or man?) would he be moved to woo? The Captain continued his lecture on the trajectory of dating.

"So we try some easy things like Scarlatti this afternoon, and then we see what happens when we get a little more deeply involved. That first Steinway was bright, fun to play around with, but gave up when the Beethoven chips were down. The second was mellow, but couldn't do bright, like to cut through an orchestra, not that you two are an orchestra. But we might gather an orchestra. The Bösendorfer was nice, but brown and too ornate for me, mien Gott. And the Baldwin was just too lightweight. With Beethoven I felt as if I was abusing some young woman. And I didn't like its previous owner. I could feel him in the cracks. Oily skin, pencil mustache. So — I haven't found her yet."

They all went back to the personal ads under "musical instruments", and a second trip down 95 took them to the University of Nevada Las Vegas, where the music department was downsizing in response to the drop in state funding since the crash. They were getting rid of two newish 6'1" Yamaha Conservatory 3s. One of them was *it*. It was her! It was she! The Captain was in love, and after a little haggling, the price was right. And it didn't take the military to bring her home. A UNLV grounds crew moved her up and into chez Warden for only 200 bucks more.

Not that a grounds crew knew how to set up a grand piano. But Bruce pulled out his iPhone, and called up an instructional video. Then three burley guys, a mesomorph, an ectomorph, and a beautiful woman all sat around and partied.

Bruce, Too, Had Been Oriented

But the orientation was in the canteen, over coffee (his) and organic orange juice (Gen. Madman's).

"You know," Madman said, confidential, "Things are seldom what they seem."

"Skim milk masquerades as cream," replied Bruce.

"Exactly. America has a Secret Destiny."

"Are you going to share the secret?"

"That's why we're here, you and I."

"And ten or fifteen others."

"Don't try to avoid me. We'll talk low. They wouldn't understand anyway. But if you and I are going to work closely together…" He took a sip of OJ.

"Ok, Sir, shoot."

"You see, we have a Constitution that's an outside wrapping, but that wrapping was planned and founded by a secret order to spread enlightenment and liberty to the world. It was no accident that God placed this continent between two oceans, to be sought out only by people with an abiding love of freedom and a unique kind of courage."

"Well, that's true," Bruce agreed. We've got the Atlantic and the Pacific."

"It's indisputable, right?"

"Roger, Sir."

"The Founding Fathers were all members of the secret society."

"So I've heard."

"You've heard right. Did you hear the story Jefferson told?"

"Which story is that, Sir?"

"About the rousing speech of the strange man who somehow got in past the locked doors of the State

House — we're talking about the Philadelphia State House — July 4th, 1776..."

"Thirteen years and twelve days before the French Revolution," Bruce noted.

"Exactly. We were way ahead of those faggot frogs. The stranger said, 'God has given it to America to be free!', as the fathers were wavering over the document. 'You've got to overcome your fears of being hanged or beheaded! You must seal your Destiny and sign this holy Contract with the Future!' So the emboldened Fathers rushed forward to sign. Hancock was closest to the table."

"Ah, that explains it."

"Listen up. When everyone had signed, they looked around for the stranger to thank him for bringing them together — but he had vanished from the room — from the locked room."

"Hm. Mysterious."

"Very. He was probably an agent of the Secret Order, guarding and guiding the Destiny of America."

"Where did you say Jefferson reported this?"

"It was in his diaries. Or his autobiography somewhere."

"Hm."

"Do you think the Secret Order would approve of what we're up to here?" Bruce asked. "I mean, not that it's a problem, but, you know, back then…"

"Captain Boynton," Madman replied, "make no mistake: America's is an implacable warrior religion. Freedom and Enlightenment are doctrines the world has yet to understand, much less practice. It's no accident that we download 'Hellfire' missiles which bring fire and brimstone to the sinful. Our Predators and Reapers are the anointed deliverers of their deaths." Further lowering his voice, practically a whisper: "And please keep all this between us. Most people can't bear too much truth. It's only we — and I include you in this, Boynton — we keepers of the Secret that can and will provide the coordinates and call the shots. We will be the judges, and if questions arise, we will secretly adjudicate them. People will take our decisions on faith. Because Americans have faith — in their country, their military, their leaders. Class dismissed."

The General took a last slug of OJ, stood, and led his companion by the elbow on to the next component of the tour.

The Course Of True Love
Never Did Run Smooth

In the following weeks the married couple were tighter than they had been in months. Perhaps it was the extended exposure to Bruce's oddities that eased them into the happy gutters of Married Life Lane, he on his side, she on hers, rolling along downslope.

One mid-summer night, Peter lay in bed watching his lovely wife undress. As he glimpsed her breasts half hidden in her golden hair, and studied her long, slim waist broadening out into a most cello-like curve of hip, his blood quickened as it always did, and the other peter rose in anticipation, creating a mountain landscape of the sheet much like that outside the bedroom window.

This night was surprisingly cool, and as Angela turned to fetch a night shirt from her drawer, a dark shape flitted across Peter's vision.

"What's that on your back?" he asked.

"It's the first draft of a tat I got down in Vegas yesterday."

"A tat?"

"A tat. A tattoo."

"You were in Vegas yesterday?"

"Yes. I forgot to tell you."

"Tell me? What about asking me?"

"I should ask permission to go to Vegas?"

"No, you should ask me what I might think about your getting a tattoo."

"OK. What do you think about my getting a tattoo?"

"I think it's barbaric. I think I don't want any bearded motorcycle thug drooling over my wife's sweet back as he needles around over her buttocks."

"OK. Next question. What do you think about my having gotten a tattoo?"

"I don't know. That's more complicated. I assume it doesn't erase."

"No. it only gets better."

"Turn around. Let me see it."

She pulled up her nightshirt, displayed her art, and wiggled her bottom at him."

"Don't do that. It's vulgar."

"Calm down. I'm just trying to make it fly."

"It? What's it?"

"It is — will be — a Sunset Morpho, *Morpho*

hecuba. Family Nymph-something. How do you like *that*? You can't make this stuff up. It will be gorgeous when it's finished. Orange and brown wings with a white starburst center, trailing black behind it. Like the slow movement of Mahler Four."

"What's Hecuba to you or you to Hecuba?", Peter asked

"Wasn't she some kind of Wiccan priestess, a witch? I don't know. I like the sound of the name. I got it to be in solidarity with the women at the Temple, the women who come through, my clients. It's like a handshake between us. They'll know they can trust me with their stories."

"More like a tailshake."

"I got it from this place." She went to the her purse, lying on a chair, and fetched out a business card.

EVE TATTOO
womynskin art from witch to bitch

On it, some nicely rendered tattoo art of Rosie the Riveter flexing a muscular arm. And on the arm, a heart-shaped earth, reading "MOM".

"So which are you," Peter asked, "witch or bitch?" By this time the mountains and hills under the sheet had been made low.

"Oh come off it," Angela laughed, "It's just a gag, a little rhyme, a spoof of logos. Everyone is really nice and laid-back down there. My artist's name is Susie, and she doesn't have a beard or drool."

"She does have a Harley, though?"

"Well, a small one. Quiet muffler."

"You've gone on a ride"

"Just around town a bit."

"You don't have a helmet."

"Suzie has two. Does the prosecution rest?"

"Did it hurt?"

"Getting the tattoo? A little bit. But Susie says the pain endings are scanty down there."

"She likes that word, 'scanty'?"

"Get off it, Peter! In case you hadn't heard, it's my body, and I'm an adult, and this is America, and I can do what I like! Jeez, all your clients have tats too. I saw them when I was there. And I'm neither a witch nor a bitch. I'm just a modern woman who loves art and beauty. I don't mind being a canvas for a three by five inch Sunset hecuba."

"It's called a tramp stamp," Peter observed.

"It isn't 'called' a tramp stamp, Angela shot back. "Certain guys, certain kinds of guys call it a tramp stamp, cause that's what they're after. Does a butterfly on my lower back mean I'm just a girl to take home to bang, a whore doing illegal drugs, stealing to support my habit? Damn, Peter, it's just a tattoo like any other, and smaller than most."

"How much did it cost?"

"Two fifty."

"$2.50?? Is that the price among sisters?"

"Two hundred fifty, idiot. I wanted a nice one. Six colors. A lot of detail. It takes time. Four sessions, she estimates."

"You're going back for more?"

"This is just the outline. Accurate. Lifted right from a Peterson Field Guide. You'll love it. And besides, it's my money."

"Your dad's money. You're a volunteer. And doctors say that it may be dangerous to give spinal anesthesia through tattoos — for women in childbirth."

"I'm forty-three years old. We're not having more children than none."

"It's still possible…" Peter offered.

"OK, let's drop it," Angela returned, playing the reluctant winner. Tomorrow, we can go to the computer, and you can see how beautiful Hecuba is."

Peter gave in, and, like his clients, decided to take it as it comes.

Perhaps it's good that musicians are often semi-illiterate. It's all that time spent practicing and playing.

Because if either Peter or Angela were more conversant with the classics, they would not have confused Hecuba with Hecate, and would know that Hecuba was not a witch or wiccan, but rather the Trojan queen, wife of Priam, king of a defeated Troy, whose weeping, known to Hamlet and quoted by Peter, was over corpses of her children, killed by Greek warriors droning death, and especially Hector dragged along through dust and over stones by Achilles' galloping chariot. All this in jealous revenge for adultery.

As Dante reports in Inferno XXX,
And when fortune overturned the pride
of the Trojans, who dared everything, so that
both the king and his kingdom were destroyed,
Poor wretched captured Hecuba,
after she saw her Polyxena dead
and found her Polydorus on the beach,
was driven mad by sorrow
and began barking like a dog...
Odysseus took Hecuba as a slave, and snarling and cursing at him, she attempted suicide. The gods took pity and turned her into a dog who spent a second life roaming with Hecate as her pet and companion. So goes one story. It was probably only a rumor. But best neither Angela nor Peter had heard it.

Sub-Plot

Desert summer turned toward desert winter. By October, the trio had gotten back into their old Berkeley groove. Wednesday nights were sacred for get-togethers, and work schedules were twisted accordingly. Increasingly, weekends began to be involved. Whatever else they did, these were musicians.

On Beethoven's 239th birthday, Bruce presented Peter and Angela with a Beethoven's 239th birthday present, and because 239 is an odd number, he made it something odd, and because it is also a prime number, he made it something never before seen or heard on planet Earth. This by oral prelude, upon presentation.

"If you're not convinced, Bruce continued, "239 is also the atomic mass of plutonium, and the number of chapters in the Book of Mormon."

Angela examined the title page of the scores in her hand.

"Three-Part Fugue from the Hammerklavier Sonata, arranged for piano trio by Captain B .F. Boynton, 432nd Wing, U.S Air Force, aka Unmanned Aerial Vehicle Battlelab."

"You...you played this at the piano tryouts," Angela said. "I mean, thank you."

"You're welcome.'

"But," she continued, "the piano already has the three parts. You don't need us."

"I've taken myself out of the upper voices, given them over to you. I can play what's left with my left hand if my right hand ever gets shot off."

"But it's so much more impressive when you play it alone." Peter said.

"Yes, but I"m 'umble. I want to hide my light under our collective basket."

"Why would you do such a thing to a master-piece?" Peter asked, almost angry. "Thank you, of course, but..."

"Because the monster is too damn complex for any human except deaf Beethoven to hear, and it's not clear he was human. This way, the ear can separate the voices, and maybe get a handle on what's going on."

"But..."

"It's an experiment. Give it a try. We can take it around to kindergartens and church groups."

They spent the evening on Bruce's gift. It actually sounded pretty good for a read-through. The voices were clearer in their entanglements, and the strings were able to sustain the longer notes, which decayed when struck by the piano. None of them had ever heard the fugue as clearly before.

By 11, Angela pled exhaustion, and dragged herself off to bed. Bruce put on his coat to leave. At the door, he turned to Peter.

"I want to tell you a secret. Come outside."

"It's cold out."

"Put on a coat."

"Just whisper it into my ear."

"Not here. The place may be bugged."

"Get away."

"Who are you talking to? Who between us knows more about bugging?"

"I do," Peter said. "We've got half the prison bugged."

"Anyway, come outside."

Peter reluctantly put on a coat, and they walked across the terrace, down the hill and looked up into the winter sky.

"So? What's up?" Peter asked.

"Did you know that there have been more than a hundred crashes of the larger class of UAVs — the

Predators, the Reapers, the Skyhawks — in over twenty countries since 2007? Did you know? No you didn't. They don't tell you this stuff. And of the smaller class, 350 pounds or less, the most common drones for surveillance, the losses are even higher."

"What's going on with them?

"I don't know. What *isn't* going on? Drones are distinctly fallible, crash-prone contraptions. Poor design, weather, mechanical failure, pilot stupidity and error, bad altitude sensors, disrupted GPS, computer glitches... Anyway, I think I know how to make a crash happen on cue."

"Yeesss?' Peter, suspicious and wary.

Bruce sat him down on a terrace chair, and pulled up another knee-to-knee. Then, in conspiratorial presto:

"And by the way, the true believer will not call them 'drones' or 'UAVs' anymore. We now call them 'Remotely Piloted Aircraft' -- 'RPAs'. Better for grunt self-esteem. But I've figured out a hack, a parallel code that can hover above and survey the drone operation and insert itself at any given prompt. Neat, huh? Surveying the surveyor? Droning the drone? Remotely piloting the remote pilot? It's Newton's Third Law. Action and reaction."

"Is this just some whacky BFB theory?"

"Wacky perhaps, but theoretical — not. It's passed

its first test. I brought down some hand-launched Ravens on cue. Three in a row.”

“What was the cue?”

“‘Turn right’, ‘turn left’, ‘turn right’. That combination.”

“How did you do that?”

“I inserted instructions into the surveying code to go into action if that combination of prompts ever occurred. No drone is too big to fail.”

Peter leaned elbows on knees, and took a moment to consider.

“Let me see if I have this right. This hovering codelet, your hack or whatever, listens in — continuously — on the operator conversations until some combination of words which it, not you, has heard, occurs. And then?”

“And then it strikes.”

“And?”

“And down comes the bird.”

“Crash, or controlled landing?”

“Controlled, mensch. It’s 10,000 bucks a shot. But it’s easy enough to code it to crash. And these Ravens crash every other launch anyway.”

Bruce stood up, and paced around the deck in tentative triumph.

“So the crashing won’t look particularly suspicious?”

"Right."

He sat down again, face to face.

"Plus I'm only a geek, not a mighty grunt. What do I know? They put up with me."

"How did you get access to the code?"

"How did I get access? I wrote the fucking thing. And I have übermensch security clearance."

"But if you wrote it, why mess around with hacking, surveying, listening for words? Aren't there easier ways to bring the thing down?"

"One, Reaper and Predator codes are a lot more complex and need complex figuring, so nothing is easy. Two, I do not believe in the Doctrine of Easiness. Three, I have become quite playful in my late years. Four, I don't want to take responsibility for any damages the deed does. As you have observed, it will be the operator who gives the cue, not I, like 'Lock on', or 'Fire'. I've never said 'Lock on' or 'Fire' in my life. You will testify to that when and if the time comes. And finally, these events should appear random, or I'll end up solitary, naked and freezing, listening to heavy metal. My plan is to use an old scheme of Groucho's. You remember 'the secret word'?"

"Where the Groucho duck comes flying in with a prize?"

"Right. The secret words will be unknowingly spoken

by the drone pilot in the course of the tracking chatter. They will be randomly selected from the fifth quintile of a list of the 5,000 most frequent words in English, that is, excluding the top 4,000 words like 'the' and 'and'. I don't want to make it too easy to win the prize, so no countdown numbers, no military commands accepted. The pilot won't know what the secret word is. Most importantly, I won't know, and I won't have selected it. They'll have to get up pretty early in the morning to sniff that spoor."

"But, Bruce, you'll be caught eventually."

"They'll have to be cleverer than they are to find my little ol' hovercraft among ten million lines of code, like those parts of DNA chains that 'don't do anything', ha ha. Moreover and even more important then my not getting caught, they need some pun-ishment that truly fits the crime of putting me here, building me into their fiendish systems to do what I do, and see what I see."

He stood up with Leninist index-finger fervor.

"They have brought this on themselves with their urge to assassinate anybody anywhere whenever. One Predator costs five million bucks. By the time they figure it out, the drone program will have gone broke, or be discontinued for unreliability. And only we will know why."

Now it was Peter who stood and peered at Bruce.

"Why are you telling me all this?"

"Because, Warden Warden, you are my friend, my confidant, my best bud, and I may need your help sometime."

"But you're putting your best bud at risk knowing this."

"When they waterboard you, I give you permission to squeal. They won't believe you, of course. But who would go after *you*, a pillar of the correctional community? I am only the harmoniumist for the fucking Baptist church!"

"But why? Why now? What?"

"I was lonely. I fell in love — with a most beautiful Pakistani girl, who unfortunately was also someone else's bride. But at my trailer orientation, I was unexpectedly invited to her Sunday wedding feast along with the guests. Music? The crew got to play the reception, buzzing away, if inaudibly, from 50,000 feet. But I could see the henna designs on her lovely face and hands."

"And?"

"And maybe one of the guests was — as they say — high-value. But I suspect they did it just to show off for me, the newbie. Five, four, three, two, one, rifle! Then 1.2 seconds for a sip of coffee, and boom. My newly beloved was no more. Nor was her husband, nor their friends at table. 'Bug splat!' my teachers cheered in unison, with high fives all around. 'Bug splat!' 'Death TV!', 'Kill 'em all, and let God sort 'em out!' 'Rock on, America!' It made me think."

"They say 'rifle', not 'fire'?"

"You bet. 'Rifle!' The better to fool themselves with."

"Hm."

"Exactly. And no one is to blame, of course, because everyone is to blame. Their lives are built on a framework designed to keep them from knowing blame. It's paradise on earth, Happyland over there."

Bruce indicated the base with a jerk of his head.

"Escape, mass murder as salvation, the way to stay in the saddle and come out as victors. The losers? The rag heads. The sand niggers. Who cares if they die? The three Fs: find, fix, and finish."

There was mutual silence in the glittering desert night. The air smelled faintly of creosote. The shadowed plants looked heavy, sharp, malevolent.

"Well what do you want me to do?" Peter offered.

"Nothing illegal or indictable. I need you as a spy, a mole."

"Doesn't sound good."

"No, it's easy. I need you to buddy up with The Madman".

An Antic Disposition: Madness But North-Northwest

One might call it nepotism, but some do have greatness thrust upon them. That was likely the case with Wilbur Lyman Creech III, commander of the Reaper Unit at the eponymous Air Force Base.

Wilbur Lyman Creech III was the 45-year old grandson of the late Gen. Wilbur Lyman Creech I , ex-commander of the U.S. Air Tactical Force, a gentleman who had previously distinguished himself over the skies of Vietnam, where he had flown 177 combat missions with a mad abandon which earned him a promotion to Asst. Deputy Chief of Staff for Operations, Headquarters Seventh Air Force, Saigon. There is a rumor (unverified) that he was the inspiration for Coppola's Col. Bill Kilgore, but while possibly detesting the smell of napalm in the morning, he was accurately recorded as saying, "Profanity is but a linguistic crutch for illiterate motherfuckers."

To distinguish him from his celebrated gaffer, "Wild Bill Creech", WLC III was fondly yclept "Madman Creech" or MC, by the underlings at the base. But Grandpa's were oversized shoes to fill, especially when MC's current activities centered not on firefights with unarmed children, but on coordinating the schedules of the nine-to-sixers manning their consoles in air-conditioned trailers set in the stillness and beauty of the Nevada desert.

Madman Creech felt he needed a psychopathology uniquely his own if he were to take his place in U.S. Air Force history. His MIT experience (ROTC, Aerospace Studies, possibly also nepotistic), combined with his haunts of the Mass Ave. bookstores and a Radcliffe girlfriend, equipped him well to initiate a new addition to DSM Chapter 9, 300.19: Factitious Disorder with Combined Psychological and Physical Signs and Symptoms — FTC, Factitious Tourette's Coprolalia.

For those not up on the latest disease or fictional character fads, Tourette's is a disorder, usually involving musculoskeletal tics — twitching, eye-blinking, shoulder-shrugging — but sometimes involving phonic symptoms — moving air through the nose, mouth or throat, as did Dickens' Mr. Pancks, "snorting and blowing" when paying attention.

Recently, books and films have featured characters exhibiting coprolalia (from the Greek, κοπροσ, feces, and λαλια, speech. Audiences love it. While only 10% of Tourette patients shittalk, authors and screenwriters have seen its money-making potential, and many people now conflate Tourette's with one low-frequency symptom. Nevertheless.

As a chosen psychopathology, it was a winner

among MC's generally coprolalic troops, exhibiting a combination of fraternal and authoritian behavior, finely titrated to make MC beloved yet obeyed.

Why "pathology" at all, rather than "effective management strategy?" Because he couldn't, or wouldn't stop it. He'd call his own mother a "maggot" to her face, and recently offended a four-star general by labeling Chelsea Manning "a slimy little Commie shit twinkle-toed cocksucker." Not politically correct.

Maj. Maureen Kranz, his then-girlfriend, advised him to see a professional,. But Gen. Wilbur Lyman Creech III rejected a staff psychiatrist referral to have his vocal cords injected with botulinum toxin to lower his volume. MC insisted volume was necessary in the pecking order, and was completely voluntary, as was his choice of diction. Behind the patient's back, Factitious Tourette's was added to the list of elective diseases by the military psychiatrist who remains unnamed to protect the identity of Patient Zero.

If anyone were capable and likely to take on the Mystery of the Fucking Mysteriously Crashing Drones" it was the Madman. And Captain Boynton knew it.

"I want to introduce you to my base commander," said Bruce to Peter. "Being a wannabe prison warden himself, he'll bask in your attention. He'll also likely consult with you about an emerging mystery, possibly a crime. I just need to know where he's at. You'll enjoy him."

Secondary Pakistan Blowback

Bruce's story, hair-raising in its entirety, was particularly piquant in one detail. Maybe he was making it up, but it sounded plausible enough in the madness that was Bruce: the idea of his falling in love with a Pakistani bride seen only by drone, transmitted halfway around the earth, a lovely young thing about to be blown to shreds. Falling in love deeply enough to risk his career, and even his life. Being lonely enough to do that.

Over the next two weeks, and especially during the next two rehearsals, Peter considered confiding in Bruce as Bruce had confided in him, and enlisting his help in a complex Peter project.

It was during a read-through of the Schubert trio they had played at their wedding. Again, that slow movement. Peter's cello began quietly, soulfully rocking in the unfathomable tenderness of the melody. When Angela entered with her treble sweetness, singing her version of the same tune, Peter's counter melody struck him for the first time as full of regret.

Regret for what? Being with her? Not being with her as he should? He needed, at some level, to find out.

Again, late enough, Angela excused herself to go off to bed, and the men were left alone. Peter took up the canonic gambit.

"I want to tell you a secret. Come outside."

Bruce picked up immediately on the fugue theme.

"It's cold out."

"Put on a coat."

"Just whisper it into my ear."

"Not here. The place may be bugged."

They laughed at the play, but something was clearly up.

CURIOUS, IMPERTINENT

"So?" Bruce asked.

"So I have this little problem," Peter admitted.

"How little? And what's the slope of its curve?"

"Dunno. But I need to talk to someone, and you're the only one I trust."

"3, 2, 1, rifle."

"Well. A couple of months ago, I brought Angela to the prison. A kind of 'take your wife to work' day...." He paused, wondering how much detail to share.

"And?"

124

"And a week or so later, Clay, my boss, the warden, showed me a note the head of security had given him."

"And?"

Peter dug his wallet out of his back pocket, fished Murillo's tattlings from among the accumulated credit cards and assorted debris, and handed the folded slip over to his friend. Bruce studied it with typical care.

"And you've been carrying this around ever since? Right in the pelvic region?"

"Well," Peter explained, "I don't think about it every day…"

"But you think about it every other day? Every third day?"

"That's about right."

"What do you think?"

"Nothing really concrete. Just about how attractive Angela is to other men…"

"Those aren't men. They're prisoners, guys who have to whack off every few hours, or copulate with cellmates after dark."

"I know, but…"

"What, you're jealous? You think they may sneak out at night and diddle our violinist behind your back?"

"No, of course not."

"They're probably not her type."

"Yes, but…"

"But what?"

"Well, we're apart all day and many evenings, and I don't know where she goes, who she eats with. I'm sure there are lots of guys out there who she affects like that, townies, soldiers, guys up from Vegas..."

"So?"

"It's not that I'm jealous of anyone in particular. It's just...I feel we've been pulling apart lately. Like how she goes off to bed alone...often. I don't know what's up. Maybe it's me. Maybe I'm inventing, projecting, who knows? But I don't feel as secure with Angela as I did."

"It's a phase, a sine wave of security-insecurity. Very common in aging marriages."

"How would you know?"

"Deduction, my man. I know from theoretical principles and a general mistrust of sine waves pretending simplicity."

"Deduction is fine for a start," Peter said, "but how about a little interlude...sonata form, ABA, an inductive development section?"

"An inductive interlude developing the theme of jealousy? Like what, cretin?"

"Captain, my Captain, how can you jeer at me like that? Even if I'm being silly or stupid, can't you see when someone is suffering? Anyone but you might take pity. Look, I would feel much more secure, much more serene, if I knew Angela was not open to enticement, not even vaguely 'available'".

"Have you asked her?"

"She'd deny it of course, and it would only raise issues…"

"Like issues are not already roiling?"

"Roiling most likely, but only in me. I'm the one who needs the Rolaids"

"And where are the Rolaids to come from?

"You, Captain."

"Me?? Listen, man, this is above my pay grade. My doctorate is in math, not woman studies."

There were people who were bad in a good way, and people who were good in a bad way, and Bruce was both. How little we've changed, Peter thought, how incredibly unlike one another we remain — though it might be our very differences that keep us friends.

"Bruce, remember when you asked me for a favor concerning Madman Creech and Project X? I'm asking for a same-level favor in return, a kind of semi-spying which might easily pass for friendship."

"Like?"

"I want you to spend some extended, unexpected time alone with Angela. I want to bug out, last minute, on the next rehearsal — call home about some emergency at work, after you're already there — and give you some time together to explore…I don't know…male/female relationships."

"You want me to go to bed with her?"

"No, no, no. Just talk — about your presumably real difficulties with women, and her thoughts about men…that kind of stuff. See if you can come up with anything interesting I can worry about. Probe. Use your devious, retentive mind. Get me evidence if you possibly can. And if you can't — that's it. That's the evidence I need. No news is great news. I can drop all this foolishness."

"If you're not there, we'll just probably play sonatas…"

"Nick your finger sharpening a pencil, whatever. You can get out of sonatas if the talk is intriguing enough."

"But if she thinks I'm coming on to her while you're gone, our trio will be kaput. And probably our friendship with it."

"You won't be coming on. You'll be discussing personal things, cementing your friendship. Family talk."

"It's true I'm not very good at coming on."

"Right. And you're as much her type as the prisoners are, on the other end of the spectrum."

"Thanks a lot."

"And being my good friend, I can trust you to not
go too far in sniffing out the goods."

TRIGGER WARNING #2

Reader, this mad plan was actually sicker than it
may appear. The fact is that Peter did have twinges
of suspicion about Angela and Bruce.

They began one night when he watched them playing the *Kreutzer Sonata* during a break from trios.
They wanted to read through the variations movement, no repeats. It was a warm night, and Angela
was wearing a camisole top innocently displaying her
beautiful arms and back.

The Kreutzer's first variation is the one Peter had
always thought of as "the tickling" one, with galloping sixteenth note triplets tickling the violin above
it, and violin occasionally scratching, and giggling
"hee, hee, hee, heee." Were they mocking him and his
unwieldy cello?

Peter was watching Angela's bare back, and twice
she hunched her shoulders as if avoiding a tickler,
and the skin shivered between the shoulder blades,
like the trembling skin of a young filly. "The Captain

tickling my wife," he thought, and laughed at his own conception.

But then, at the end, Angela said, "Let's just get into the last movement," and for a minute, they danced away together, presto, in a singing tarantella. Away from him…together.

"OK, enough," Bruce said, needing a break, and not wanting to further subtract from the trios.

Peter was unaccountably upset. And they hadn't even visited the fiery, passionate first movement.

During a pee break, he meditated on the event. They played very beautifully. There, in front of him, had been two excellent musicians exercising their noble art together. Yes, together, he and she. Bruce and Angela. And Peter felt clumsy. No one but a stupid, jealous husband would think anything blameworthy about it. But he knew, he had experienced, how music leads to thoughts of love, and the sinuous twining of counterpoint often leads to the sensuous twining of bodies.

Were they both hypnotized by Ludwig van? If so, what were the post-hypnotic suggestions of that frustrated lover? *An die ferne Geliebte*? Was all the musical tickling and passion calling Bruce and Angela vaguely forth into some secret life?

It was preposterous, of course, that a 10+ woman

would fall for a -3 man. What a mismatch! Still, there was much in Bruce to admire, much that Peter could not boast. His phenomenal intellect and musical memory, his command of twenty, thirty times as many notes per piece as they had to deal with. Peter had seen beautiful women with ugly men, and vice versa. He didn't understand it, of course. Did that make him superficial, placing so much value on appearance? Angela and Bruce. It could be.

And so, his request of Bruce to test Angela had a hidden dimension: it was at the same time a setup for Angela to test Bruce. He would quiz them both separately, afterwards. If she found anything uncomfortable, he was sure she'd tell him. And then he laughed. What could be funnier than unwarranted suspicions? But that was exactly what he was having, and half his strength for the rest of the evening was spent in not letting anyone notice.

FRIENDLY ADVICE

"…I can trust you to not go too far in sniffing out the goods."

"My friend," Bruce said, "Listen up. You have no facts announcing infidelity. I do understand that facts are not the same as truth. And that the legal, factual lack of proof is not a vector indicator of direction. You doubt, period. It's the human condition since Descartes.

"And people do betray one another. That's a tradition going back to Adam and Eve. There is a series A,B,A,B,A,B…betrayal A, immediately followed by betrayal B, then A again, receding into infinity.

"Within this, you are lucky: you are loved. But please realize that there are other people who *aren't* loved. Have you ever thought about *them*? How do they handle it? You think Angela might be unfaithful, and ready to betray you? But what can she betray, except her love for you? She can't betray *not* loving you. Ergo, she loves you. You are loved. So don't smother your wife with your own suffering. When she turns blue, you'll stop loving her.

"Point number two begins with a quiz. Ready?"

"I suppose…"

"How many people do you think there are in a heterosexual marriage, and no, you're wrong: there are *three* people — the woman, W, the man, M, and the most important person, WM, the amalgam of the man and the woman together. If one of the people commit adultery, the person who is most deeply hurt is WM, the two-in-one.

"So ease up, Don Carlos. You're only the designated patient here, not the real one.

"Nevertheless, I will have an extended personal talk with Angela, as you suggest. I will even nick a finger, if necessary, to assure we have some time. Why? Because she's very sexy, I've always liked her, I think I might learn something, and I owe you one."

MATH IS TRUTH — FOR SOME

When in doubt, Bruce thought, trust mathematics. How can first-order predicate logic go wrong? It'll never fail. Relations between quantities. Their rates of change. Tattooed on God's arm. When all else fails, and the stone has crushed you at the bottom of the hill, you can huff up and regroup around mathematics.

Peter is far too romantic. He needs more math in his life. Something independent of sticky emotionalism. Rubenstein, Toscanini. The syllogism, the identity. God's cookbook.

Sophocles may be mortal, but mathematics is immortal.

THE PSYCHOPATHOLOGY OF CREATIVE PEOPLE

We observe that many wonderful, creative people — and most acknowledged geniuses — are eccentric. Researchers, (those who are likely less so), seem to think that this valuable cohort suffers from a diminished ability to filter things out in their cognitive stream. Their brains have to deal with more sounds, more images, more ideas than those of average persons. Consequently they need to metabolize, process, organize and excrete all this information in their own, atypical ways. It's a pain.

"Ah, reduced dopamine," you may say. "Reduced dopamine binding in the thalamus. That must be it. Reduced dopamine can suffocate filtering and stimulate cognitive disinhibition." Perhaps you are right. Less dopamine, fewer dopes.

It may be that Peter's issues stemmed from reduced dopamine. Why else would he notice the slight quivering between his wife's shoulder blades when being trilled at by Beethoven and/or her lover? Perhaps a little dopamine, daily, sprinkled on his Familia, or in his morning coffee would do the trick.

Bruce, on the other hand, was beyond such treatment.

Robert Heinlein, author of *Stranger in a Strange Land*, sci-fi guru to both gentlemen's youths, once wrote, "A human being should be able to change a diaper, plan an invasion, butcher a hog, conn a ship, design a building, write a sonnet, balance accounts, build a wall, set a bone, comfort the dying, take orders, give orders, cooperate, act alone, solve equations, analyze a new problem, pitch manure, program a computer, cook a tasty meal, fight efficiently, die gallantly. Specialization is for insects." Captain Bruce F. Boynton could do none of these except solve an equation. And, if one were less than generous, one might even say he approximated an insect more than a human, with his coke-bottle glasses, bent spine, cachectic figure, and irritating voice.

If anything could save his human beingness, it was his accumulation of eccentricities. Even his eccentricities were eccentric:

- Beethoven's personal habits were suspect; Bruce brushed his teeth six times a day.
- Howard Hughes had a allegedly germ-free suite of rooms in the Beverly Hills Hotel for when he would spend his days indoors; Bruce would eat anything off the floor — which perhaps accounts for his tooth-brushing.
- Einstein picked up cigarette butts off the street to snarf tobacco for his pipe; Bruce would use only a hookah, and who knows what was in it?
- Ben Franklin was a nudist; BFB would never take off his clothes in public, even for doctors or gym teachers.
- Erik Satie ate only white foods; Bruce barely ate at all.
- Nikola Tesla fed pigeons and would flex his toes

100 times every night to stimulate his brain; Bruce
detested pigeons, would carry a water pistol if he
was to be around them, and didn't need toe flexing. In fact, he could barely sleep at night from
plotting-brain syndrome.

- Jesus's silence was too much for the Grand
  Inquisitor; Bruce was inordinately logorrheic.

But the panacea for all his pathologies was music.
Especially Schubert. He could get inside the songs,
reveling in a world where sorrow was undeniable and
laughter genuine, where songs hated and loved with
all their souls, where people danced with joy, and love
was not cynical, where values remained, free from
havoc and ruination.

A word, though, about his Don Carlos crack. What
could he have been thinking of? What could he have
been warning his friend about? What, in the worst
case, could he have been predicting? For musicians,
two possibilities come to mind, neither very upbeat.
In anti-chronological order they are:

1. Verdi's opera, *Don Carlos* (1883). Two virtuous, beautiful women, two virtuous, handsome men.
At the end, Carlos and his old friend Posa are dead or
about to be, enveloped by a complex plot of jealousy,
secret beloveds, an unloved king, a wronged wife,

suspicion, confusion, and deceit.

2. Don Carlo Gesualdo, Prince of Venosa, inspired composer, maniac and murderer. In 1590, in a Napoli palace, premeditated, assisted by his secret service, he murdered his wife and her lover *in flagrante delicto*, and left their bloody bodies on the front steps, her corpse to be raped by a monk, and the lover's to be eaten by dogs. Or so they say. One listen to his late madrigals would make the case, QED.

A Renaissance historian might say that the Gesualdo porn has been overblown, and that such murders lay well within the morality of the high Renaissance. The Prince may have had little choice but to do what he did — his reputation, his family's, and his court's, could not be maintained were he an unavenged cuckold. Besides, he could get away with it. The buck stopped at his desk. His world would excuse the frantic actions of a romantic, brilliant young man. And, according to the latest research, his wife, horrified at being discovered, may have died by her own hand.

Bruce was a great fan of Gesualdo — his music and his murders.

But neither 1) nor 2) was good news. Perhaps the Captain was referring to something else entirely.

Meanwhile, On The Other Side Of The Pond

At almost the same moment as the above late-night Nevada conversation between Peter and Bruce occurred, that is, around 8:30AM, Amiens time, Cybèle LaPieux and Alan Newberry strolled hand in hand, the lock in his, the keys in hers, to the beautiful little bridge over the St.-Lieu Canal in the Place du Don, a block north of the cathedral.

They were there to place the first "love-lock" on that little bridge, taking a cue from the bridges over the Seine whose railings are now buckling with the weight of love. *Cadenas d'amour.* Their pledge, a Cogex 80104 with two keys bought at Monsieur Bricolage for €3,5, seeded a flood of similar attestations from lovers in the Somme now numbering in the high hundreds. It was engraved by Jean Delatour, and it said, "Alan and Cybèle FOREVER." They placed and fastened it on the middle section of railing, she took one key, he the other, and they strolled a block further south to kiss the keys, kiss each other, and each throw them into the flowing Somme, never to be used again. *Geste charmant.*

Charming, but non-predictive.

They had met after an event at the great cathedral at which Cybèle's *ensemble vocal* from the Lycée Sacré Coeur had given its annual concert, ending with Josquin's *Ave Maria*. After disappearing into the green room off the chancel to change, she returned to find Alan waiting for her.

"Pardon," he said, *"tu t'appelles Marie?"*

He was cute. She thought she'd play along. But not so much as to answer this obvious American in French.

"Yes," she said. "Why? Do I know you? How did you know I call myself Mary?"

"Because you were in blue, and full of grace. I loved watching you sing."

It stank of a specialized pickup line, but at least he understood Latin. Or maybe he was Catholic, old style. Or maybe a translation was in the program.

They walked down the north transept toward the door.

"John the Baptist's head is in there," he said, pointing at a reliquary on the wall.

"You study the guidebook," she noted.

"No, just a brochure."

Honest? Self-effacing? Cute, anyway.

"May I walk you home?"

"I live at the school. The Lycée Sacré Coeur. My name isn't Mary, it's Cybèle."

"Oh," he said, surprised. But he wouldn't press it. "My name is Alan."

She always called him "Alain."

Oil And Water

Cybèle and Alain. Cute.

But not so cute was the note Peter found at his lockup, nine hours later, on a hot Nevada morning under the brutal and businesslike sun.

In his mailbox, scrawled on paper with the same black ballpoint, on the same lined note pad, Peter found the following: SEE ME — MURILLO. It struck him as odd that the signature lacked Murillo's title, which he insisted on at every turn. And then it seemed even odder — perhaps even improper — that the note was not addressed to him, either by name or by title. He was Murillo's superior, wasn't he? Or was he? Actually, he didn't know the lateral chain of command among Warden Straud's subordinates. In any case, its tone was nasty, curt, rude, disrespectful, a note that might be written by a principal to a teacher who had done something politically incorrect in class.

Peter knocked on the "Head of Security" door, with its window of wired glass. Murillo, on the phone, waved him in, then waved him to a chair. Peter sat while he finished up his call, and tried to analyze the power situation he was in, planning his performance in a duet coming up more complex than Ravel.

"Lt. Murillo…" Peter began.

"You can cut the title. We're behind closed doors. It's Frank."

"All right. Then it's Peter. I came because…"

"I know why you came. But I'm not sure *you* do. Look, we haven't really had a talk since you've come, and we've been stalking each other at a distance…"

"I'm not stalking you," Peter averred.

"Well, I've been stalking you."

"Why is that?"

"To protect you, hombre. I have to know all about you, about what you're up to -- to protect you. I'm head of security, right? And that includes your security. So I need to give you some friendly advice. I'm your friend whether you think so or not. And I know what's going on — everywhere. I'm on the inside more than you, I'm on the yard more than you, and in the halls and the corridors and the decks and the walkways. I talk to my enemies cause they have to talk to me. And I talk to my buddies. So I know what I'm talking about."

"OK. Go on." The duet was turning into a solo with audience.

"You're in trouble, man. With both sides. There's a staff revolt brewing, and the prisoners are using you, mocking you, and excuse the language, fucking with you."

This was news to Peter, who surely thought himself the most popular of the staff, an effective programs visionary and a regular guy, even though a good friend of the warden's. Many men signed up to be in his programs. But perhaps all was not as copacetic as he thought. An ominous trill began to crescendo.

"Pete, I know you haven't come up through the ranks like I have, and I know that corrections theory and practice often diverge. I'm not a dummy. But even here at shiny, new HDSP there's a traditional, functional, caste system evolved over centuries from trial and practice, built by administrators, bulls, and cons. And you're pushing on it with your "therapeutic community" stuff, your art and poetry workshops and your theater games."

"You mind if I get a word in?" Peter asked.

"I know what you're going to say. I know the theory and the rationale. But go ahead and say it."

"Look, Frank. There's good data that men in these programs have reduced recidivism. Substantially lower. Lower by half. In the theater programs, recidivism is down to less than 10% for return within three years."

"Yeah, but what about three years and a month, or four years or five? In my orientations, I see the same faces coming up over and over again. The old guys die off, and their places are filled in from the bottom by the punks. You want to know what a con told me yesterday on the yard? He said you remind him of a broad with all your politeness and gentleness. He said he'd like to fuck you. In the ass. And the guys around him laughed, and said 'Yeah, go for it!' And you know what I heard about the theater program specifically? That it's part of our punishment agenda. That it's a pacifier to help me with my job. That nobody likes prison riots, especially the politicians up in Carson City, and the fat cats in Reno, and you and your programs are keeping disturbances down, and lib-washing our image. People out there think we're rehabilitating, when we're not. And some prisoners have told me you're giving them emotional pain with your exercises."

"And what's with the staff?" Peter glumly asked.

"They feel threatened by your programs, by prisoners who get used to 'expressing themselves', who are encouraged to 'feel free' in their art and poems and skits. 'You rehearse them for revolt,' they say. You 'improve their acting so they can better lie and deceive us.' There's some real resentment cooking there."

"These prisoners are all human beings."

"They're human, but they and we belong to different castes, we've internalized different caste behaviors. They have only each other to show off for and count on. And you're trying to change that."

"I am."

"Look, we're safe, and so the public is safe, but only if we're kept apart. That's why the men are here, that's why they're behind bars at night. These guys are losers. Over and over. You can't change them. Most of them even like it here. Three hots and a cot and in-house sex, no sweat. If it were up to me, and we had enough space, I'd have them all in seg, and throw away the key. But we have to work within the regs. That's what we're asking them to do, and when we — you— ignore the regs, even if it makes our jobs easier, then we're only showing them we're no better than they are. My major interest is in running a trouble-free, smooth institution, one that doesn't get into the newspapers because of riots."

"OK, Frank." Peter said. "Point taken. Thanks for sharing." And he walked to the door.

"Pete," Murillo said.

"Yeah?"

"You've been warned. Watch your ass."

Three + One Possibly = Four

"A nice young girl came by today," Angela told Peter You'd like her. She's a singer, French."

"Hmm," Peter grunted. "What's she doing here?"

"She came to the temple, looking for housing. Ran away from an American husband in DC who was beating on her. That's confidential."

"Can you help her?"

"She's in the Maiden Room at the guest house."

"Is she a maiden?"

"Who knows — with a battering husband? It was the only room open."

"If she's lonely, have her over for dinner some night. Or maybe we can make some music with her and the Captain."

"Good idea. Like what?"

"What's her voice?"

"I don't know. Alto, mezzo, from her speech."

"Does she sight sing?"

"She was in a performing choir. They sang at Amiens Cathedral."

"Let me think about what we might do."

Think about it he did. And he recalled an experience from thirty years back, when Bidu Sayao had come to Cornell. He remembered her being old, but beautiful — and scary. She had sung something by a Frenchman who went insane. His dad told him that. Ravel, maybe. Didn't he go insane?

A little googling, and there it was. The *Chansons Madecasses*. Piano, mezzo-soprano, cello, and clarinet — which his father had played at that faculty concert. And he thought it was a fierce political piece, anti-imperialist. Child Peter didn't know what that meant. But he wrote it down.

A Strange Event In The Chapel

Weekly worship services are offered in one of the two chapels at Creech Air Force Base. Denominations represented include Catholic, Protestant, Jewish and Islamic religions. The Protestant chaplain had made room for a guest speaker, his colleague, Gen. Wilbur Lyman Creech III, lay minister, so he claimed, of the All Souls Interfaith Life Church, whatever that was.

Left of the altar in the A-frame chapel, Bruce seated himself at the Hammond. After announcements, and Joys and Concerns, Gen. Creech began innocuously enough:

"I want to thank you all for coming even though the Rev. Cody is AWOL today. Emergency family business. But though I am a goddam poor substitute, I have a team of top-flight lunatics at my back "

The worshippers knew they were in for a trip.

"Say ye to the righteous, it shall be well with him: for they shall eat the fruit of their doings.

"But woe unto the wicked! It shall be ill with him: for the reward of his hands shall be given him.

"Behold, my servants shall sing for joy of heart, but ye shall cry for sorrow of heart and shall howl for vexation of spirit."

The quotation came out of the blue, entirely unprepared by the previous remarks. Furthermore, Creech's voice had taken on a new quality -- or was it his voice at all? The closest approximation was the disembodied voice heard at all hours of the day and night over the base PA system, but here shorn of its electronic quality.

Bruce felt his heart speeding up, and a sweat breaking out on his upper lip. Did Creech know about his rebellion? Was he going to expose him as the Reaper reaper? Would he be lynched by the sanctimonious grunts who flew them?

"These are the words," Creech continued, "of First Isaiah, who began to preach in the reign of King Uzziah, in the eighth century BC, before you were born. First Isaiah was a visionary moralist, calling upon a country in the summit of its power. In Jerusalem the IDF was deploying engines on each of its towers, high-tech weapons capable of shooting arrows long distances, and heaving great stones."

Murmuring and buddy-buddy approval in the congregation.

"In the year that King Uzziah died, First Isaiah had a vision: he saw the Lord sitting upon a throne, high and lifted up. Above the throne stood the seraphim, and each one had six wings; and with two they covered God's face, with two they covered His feet, and with two they flew — insect-like angels, shielding men from the radiation of God. They could scare the crap out of anyone."

Radiation? The radiation of God? Did the madman know something about the program Bruce didn't?

"Because whatever the pussies among you may think, politics is based on the power of the sword. That's you.

"Now all of you know some of First Isaiah's words, and being warriors, you've laughed at them. He announced a day when nations 'shall beat their swords into plowshares and their spears into pruning hooks.' Are you smirkers still listening? First Isaiah proclaimed the day when nation shall not lift up sword against nation, neither shall they learn war any more."

It had become clear that this was to be no short, standard speech from the religion Division. Some in the audience of thirty or so became restless, some transfixed. The grunts knew they could not leave, and Peter and Angela would certainly not have abandoned them. They too were skewered in.

"Now hear this, friends:

Creech III paused to let the next sink in.

Woe unto them that call evil good, and good evil; that put darkness for light, and light for darkness; that put bitter for sweet, and sweet for bitter!

Woe unto them that are wise in their own eyes, and prudent in their own sight!

Woe unto them that follow strong drink, that continue till night, till the wine inflame them! And the harp, and the viol, the tabret, and pipe are in their feasts: but they regard not the work of the Lord, neither consider the operations of his hands.

By now Peter and Angela were tachycardic, he because of his nightly martinis, and both of them because of the viols, tablets and pipes.

"Please open your hymnbooks to Hymn number 65. It's about you.

Day of wrath! O day of mourning!
See fulfilled the prophets' warning,
Heav'n and earth in ashes burning!
O what fear man's bosom rendeth,
When from heaven the Judge descendeth,
On Whose sentence all dependeth.

The singing was your usual congregational monotonic mumbling — especially given the unfamiliar hymns. But Creech counted on the words sinking in with whomever his targets were.

"Howl ye! for the day of the Lord is at hand," the Madman yelled in a voice from nowhere and from everywhere.

"God's call was for Plan R: decimation! First Isaiah was assigned to cover the news. Reduce stiff-necked Israel to a remnant, let things begin again. And the Jews were scattered, and their Temple destroyed."

He paused. Where could he be going?

"We will now take up the collection."

Bruce improvised as he did for the Baptists, but this time with his hands shaking. He brewed up a choral prelude based on the Air Force Song: Down we dive, spouting our flame from under….Off with one helluva roar….We live in fame or go down in flame…Nothing'll stop the Army Air Corps! The chorale phrases were spaced so far apart that no one but Peter or Angela could possibly pick up on the scheme, and Angela had never even heard the Air Force Song. Between the phrases, Messiaenic organ rumbles and flights. It was quite an unnerving composition, never, thank goodness, to be repeated.

Things were truly uncomfortable. This kind of stuff might have gone over at the First Baptist Church of Indian Springs, but this was the 432nd Air Wing Chapel. Madman Creech 3 seemed to sense this, and pulled back. After the plate had been passed, he continued.

"Let me say a few words about history. This is what the prophets discovered: History is a clusterfuck nightmare. We all assume that politics, economics, and warfare are the substance of history. Well, bullshit. For the prophets, it is God's judgement of man which is the big deal."

Bruce thought maybe this whole thing was not, after all, directed at him. Peter and Angela looked around surreptitiously, trying to gauge their neighbors' reactions.

"Two centuries and a half ago, we opted for freedom. It was a right decision; it created something new and great in history. But we excluded the security without which man cannot live and grow. And now the quest for security splits the whole world with demonic power.

"But what in the world are we making? Wars, victories, more wars. So many tears. So little regret. And who can sit in judgement when victims' horror turns to hate? What can save us is only man's capacity – your capacity -- for repentance. But something stands in the way. Do you know what that is? What stands in the way of repentance is the worship of power. Why are you all so ready to kill and die at the call of kings and chieftains, presidents and generals? It is because you worship power, you think it is by might that man prevails."

Creech III's between-the-lines was growing ominous, and Peter, once again, felt accused for his power over his captives.

"Now as then, the sword is the pride of man, and now it is our drones which lend supremacy to nations. War is the climax of human ingenuity, the object of supreme efforts; men slaughtering each other, cities and settlements blown to ruins. What is left behind? Agony and desolation. And a spirit of revenge."

Creech looked around, fixing every pair of eyes in the congregation.

"You think very highly of yourselves, don't you? You are wise in your own hearts and shrewd in your own sight.

"Seems inconceivable, doesn't it? Swords to ploughshares? War to be abolished? You shall not learn war any more because you shall seek other knowledge. Your hearts of stone will melt. Are you ready for the switcheroo?"

Two officers got up disgustedly to leave, making a lot of noise along the way. Creech ignored them.

"War abolished? Happy ending? Nice and tidy? But the Bible is not shallow like you." The madman paused again to gauge those who remained. The ensuing tension produced only the disembodied voice again:

Woe to those who call evil good and good evil,
Who put darkness for light and light for darkness!
Woe to him who builds a town with blood,
And founds a city on iniquity.

Chaplin Creech sat down to indicate that his strange sermon was over.

Bruce, confused, hands more than shaking, began the usual recessional of Onward, Christian Soldiers. Scooting from chancel to rear, Madman was at the door to greet the men as they exited. Peter and Angela hung at the organ — "clung" might be a better description — and listened to Bruce vocalize, in Brechtian Sprechstimme style,

At the sign of triumph Satan's host doth flee;
on then, Christian soldiers, on to victoree!
Hell's foundations quiver at the shout of praise;
brothers, lift your voi-oi-ce-es, loud your anthems raise.

"Love that verse," Bruce darkly explained. He finished the last refrain with a sustained Ivesian cadence — which alone made them all quiver — and the three of them tottered down the nave together toward the door.

"Gen. Creech," Bruce said, "I'd like you to meet my friends, Peter and Angela. We play music together."

"Nice to meet you, Nice to meet you," as if nothing extraordinary had gone on. But Madman was sizing the trio up with laser vision. Peter felt it. Bruce felt it. Angela felt it, and shivered.

They all three concluded they were dealing with a very loose cannon.

First Meeting Of A New Four

Again:

"Nice to meet you."

"Nice to meet you."

"Very nice to meet you."

Innocent beginning.

How did Cybèle arrive at Sekhmet?

By thumb.

She was staying in The Maiden Room. Was she still a maiden?

Surprisingly, she was. Very clever, these Catholic schools. You pound religion into young women's heads, season it with fear of hell, with archaic notions of right and wrong, you get them to equate servility with love, and rebellion with sin. It can work, though it gets ever more difficult. But in Cybèle's case it was irrelevant. That is, it was not Sacré-Coeur-Amiens that had kept her a virgin at age 18. It was her older two brothers, Bernard and Denis, who had so misused her once she had started growing breasts and a bit before, that even the vocabulary of her Married Life class, the very words *"paroi vaginale"*, *"entrant"*, *"pénétration"*, *"testicules"*, *"engorgé"* made her gag. Visceral dread. Helpless disgust at being touched down there. Or even thinking about it.

Try as they might to score, she fought her brothers like a fury, and they never got beyond third base. They threatened to kill her if she told, and to swear she put out even though she didn't.

She resisted penetration over four years of wary weekends, sleeping in the same house with her frères. pretending to Papa and Maman that all was well, but living in fear of defilement and discovery. Several times, they snuck into her dorm to teach her that even the Sacré-Coeur might not protect her. When she screamed, they skedaddled.

She wanted out, and far away. It was easy to understand why she eloped with the first foreigner who seemed acceptable. Cybèle and Alain. Cute.

Such courage and strength from an elfin girl with dancing feet and singing voice, more vibrational than solid, whom one might well suspect of being a child brought by fairies.

Rape is not just an act — it robs one of a life. it determines an existence incapable of trust, wary of intimacy. It makes sex an object of obsessive thought, but never enjoyment. All Cybèle could think about was avoidance.

In New York on her wedding night, she discovered that her new husband did not share her horror of "penetration". For her, the act of love was a region of corruption and vice. What he had virtuously awaited, she now denied. One night, two nights, a week, her soul engaged in unrelenting combat. And that was quite enough for him. He was no saint. He claimed his "rights". He yelled and hit her, forced her down, and spread her legs. The next morning, she was gone. And still a maiden.

What was the first thing the new four of them did together?

Test her English and their French. All passed. Plans for being in the U.S.? A "tourist visa".

And then?

And then she remarked on the beautiful piano, on the violin lying upon it, on the cello case standing nearby. They talked about her music and theirs, and the music at the great cathedral. What had she sung? What did she love, and why? Bruce joked about his church jobs. and told her about Schubert at the wedding.

"Do you know Ravel's *Chansons Madecasses?*" Peter asked.

"Actually, yes," she said. "I heard it in the Cathedral. Soeur Aline assigned to us to study the text."

"Soeur Aline was your music teacher?" Angela asked.

"No," Cybèle said. "She taught to us French history, and *Chansons Madecasses* was concerning of colonization. I mean it was in the study of colonization."

Neither Bruce nor Angela knew the piece. "Why is that?" Bruce asked.

"Madegascar," Peter said. "It's about Madegascar."

"I don't know much about Madegascar," Angela admitted.

"Off southeast Africa," Peter informed them, "an island in the Indian Ocean. The French took it over, end of the 19th century."

"By much of violence," Cybèle added. "The Madegascars made a Resistance."

"So this poet, what was his name?"

"Évariste de Parny," Cybèle put in.

"Right. De Parny wrote some poems in the 1920s, and Ravel…"

"*Attendez, attendez,* wait." said the guest. "De Parny wrote the poems at the end of the eighteenth century, around our Revolution, except he was in India. And he said he gathered together the poems, like folk poems, but I think he wrote some of them. This was before the French come, *mais l'esprit…*"

"Interesting," Peter said, "I didn't realize… Anyway Ravel picked three of the poems to set. Provocative subject matter. Wild, emotional music. You know Ravel." He winked at Angela.

"You want to play this, all of us together?" Cybèle asked.

Peter nodded.

"But there is the clarinet. Who will play clarinet?" Cybèle asked.

"Angela can play the part on violin. I'll transpose it up a step. I think it will sound fine. She's good."

"Oh yes, yes, I'm sure, but…I don't know if my voice will be strong enough or I can make all the notes."

"We'll see, *n'est-ce pas?*" Bruce said. "Sounds like fun. With some anti-imperial energy for dessert."

Angela would order the parts from New York, Peter would make the transposition. Bruce didn't want to peek. He'd try to sight read it, first rehearsal.

Did Cybèle's difficult personal path ever come up?

No. Sekhmet's client confidentiality.

WORKOUT

"Er....General? Gen. Creech?

Madman lay on a bench, hands at his chest, gripping a bar loaded with half a dozen huge weights. He paid no attention to his visitor.

"Thirty nine...forty..." as the burden went up and down, punctuated by huge breaths.

"Gen. Creech, excuse me, but Gen. Trockler said I could talk to you in the gym."

"Forty-five...forty-six....Just wait till I finish this set...forty-seven...You can spot me...forty-eight... Get behind there...forty-nine...fifty." He dropped the bar onto the rack over his head. "You didn't spot me," he said, only slightly out of breath.

"Well, I...I couldn't really..."

"Of course, you couldn't, Boynton. I wouldn't trust you anyway, with those arms. How big are your arms, Captain?

"I don't know, sir. I never..."

"Ambler, get over here," he yelled to one of the

other soldiers in the gym. Bring a tape. On the double." Sgt. Ambler came trotting over looking like an over-muscled tailor in strange clothing. "Measure the captain's bicep, Ambler. Boynton, make a muscle...a muscle, soldier. Bend your arm, make a fist, flex."

Bruce had never assumed that position in his life, though his arms and back were surprisingly strong from late Beethoven.

"Thirteen and three-quarter inches, sir," the sergeant reported.

"Now measure mine," the sleeveless madman ordered. He flexed his right bicep, and grimaced.

"Twenty inches, sir, and a quarter.."

"Dismissed, sergeant. Go work on your abs. A little flab there."

"Yes, sir."

Ambler trotted back to his iron pile.

"What is it you want, Captain?"

"I don't mean to interrupt you when you're working out, sir, but..."

"It's fine, Boynton, fine. I like my men to see me at my best. Keeps them in their place."

"I went to your office, and Gen. Trockler said you were working out, and that it would be perfectly ok to see you in the gym..."

"I told you it's fine, soldier. So what do you want?"

"Well, I was just reading the *Air Force Times*, an article on rape culture in the military, a Pentagon report, and I was wondering..."

"You got a problem with rape culture, Boynton, with those thirteen inch arms?"

"The article said there were 15,000 incidents reported last year, and probably a lot more unreported, and I was wondering..."

"Does that go on here in Funland? Sure it does. Why not? Why shouldn't it? I wish there were more — per capita. We're low on the list, Captain, but that's because a lot of our men get their rocks off on their wives every night when they go home. By and large, the men — and women — at Creech do not rape. We need more single men on base to get our rape numbers up. But don't worry. All is well. My boys fuck hard."

Was he putting Bruce on?

"Sir, I remember a sermon of yours I attended, where you talked about the evils of worshipping power, about nourishing peace..."

"That ye may suck, and be satisfied with the breasts of her consolations...Did you notice that part, or did I leave it out? Lemme do another set."

The curious nature of this man was a conundrum. The madman held forth between presses.

164

"Capt. Boynton, we're in a war. Six. Lots of wars. Seven. More to come. Eight. In wars, aggressiveness is the key to victory, compassion is the slippery slope to defeat. Nine. Violence is our language, get it? Ten. Peace is for the weak, war is for the strong."

"But in your sermon, you said…"

"I know what I said. That's what I believe."

The bar rested back on the stand.

"But sir, these women…they're part of the military. They've given up a regular life to serve their country, place themselves in harm's way…"

"Not here, they don't."

"How can you…"

"Look, Boynton. Some groups of people are simply inferior to other groups. It wasn't in the sermon, but people have to take their proper places, assume the position, if you get my meaning. Sometimes it's necessary to use force. Some are slayers, some are slain. Which side do you want to be on? What better reason for our splendid array of weapons? In Jesus' name.

"It would be good if all groups could be equal. Sure. Group equality should be our ideal. All groups should be given an equal chance. But this is war, Boynton. Some groups need to triumph over others. And it's not going to be the slits or the rag heads. Or the women.

Why do you bring this up? Need some instruction on what to do with those thirteen inch arms at night?"

"Well, sir, I have a friend, one of the wardens at the prison."

General Creech sat up on the press bench.

"And?"

"Actually, you met him with me after your sermon. Peter Warden."

"Peter Warden? Warden Warden? Is he the one with the beautiful broad?"

"I guess you could say that. Angela, his wife."

"I'd like to launch my missile into her."

"Yes sir. So would many others. The thing is that Peter mentioned similar problems with the prisoners, and…

"They don't mix the men and women over there."

"Men rape one another, and a lot of them are in for crimes of sexual violence."

"It's not the same thing. Not even similar. Those people are losers. Our men are winners. Those men are scum of the earth. Ours are, or should be, the cream of humanity. Violence against women, them and us — two different things, two different purposes, two different results."

"OK. But I was just wondering if you'd like to get together with Peter to share your takes on the issue. Your different takes, to be sure."

"Will what's her name be there? Angela?"

"I suppose — if we do it at their house."

"Make a fucking appointment. I'll be there. Let me know. Anything else?"

"Sir, do you mind if I ask a personal question?"

"Of course not. Go right ahead. I like to be open with my men. I have nothing to hide."

"Why do you work out so much? Pump iron, as they say?"

"Well, for one, I want to top that Kraut governor. What did we win the war for? He's had twenty-two inch arms, and mine are only twenty."

"And a quarter," Bruce added, consoling.

"His chest, top form, was fifty-seven inches, and mine is only fifty-two. So I've got a ways to go. Can't let the Krauts snatch victory from the jaws of defeat."

"So that's why you spend hours…"

"If you want the real secret, Boynton, and you can apply it to yourself, the real secret is qualitative, not quantitative. You called this pumping iron. But iron is only a path — to steel. Steel, Boynton, steel is beyond iron. Iron is just an element, but steel is a creation of the human spirit. I'm pursuing the Secret of Steel."

"And what's that?" Bruce asked, glad he asked, and genuinely intrigued.

"Do you know anything about the Bessemer Process?"

"I've heard of it, but actually, no."

"The Bessemer process uses oxygen blown through the molten pig iron to burn off the impurities. Then an exact amount of carbon and magnesium is added to create steel."

"Like nutritional supplements," Bruce remarked.

"Like nutritional supplements, exactly," Madman confirmed. "I take a lot of them. Over one hundred pills a day. Plus shakes. Plus morning prayer. To shield me.

"But the key is getting rid of impurities. Our health care, especially the military's, doesn't seem to give two shits about how impure, pollutant, toxic metals build up in our food, water, drugs, vaccines, in our homes and our bodies, and slowly but surely lead to disease and civilization decay. The more metals build up in our brains, the more we become antenna-like, the more pushed around by enemy-made electromagnetic fields in our environment — getting worse by the day. EMFs suppress the immune system and weaken the blood-brain barrier, and lead to further eroding our resistance to toxins. Where do you think all these new learning disabilities come from?"

"That sounds a lot like what's his name's take in *Strangelove*. Precious bodily fluids. Purity of essence."

"General Ripper's. Of course it does. Stanley Kubrick was an initiate. All his films send coded messages about The Wisdom, the IS. *2001, Full Metal Jacket, Clockwork Orange, The Shining* — You think these are about what they're "about"? They're a shoutout to the brotherhood cleverly disguised as satire. Subtle solidarity. Subliminal seeding. You just have to know in order to know."

"I've seen those films a lot, and I never…"

"Of course you never. You don't think — you're just logical. You know, we got off the track when we let our government go secular, when we stopped understanding that God created this nation, that He wrote the Constitution, that it's got to be firmly based on biblical principles. And it's we, here at Supertown, that have to lead the nation back to the noble eight-fold path."

"Which is?"

"Which is right view, right intention, right speech, right action, right livelihood, right effort, right mindfulness, right concentration. What are you, Jewish or something, you don't know that? What do they teach you in math school?

"And what is right action? War, my friend. War is right action. The Lord is a warrior. In Revelation 19 it says when he comes back, he's coming back leading a mighty army, riding a white horse with a white robe stained with enemy blood. He's coming back as a bar-

barian carrying a sword. And I believe - I've checked this out - I believe that 'sword' he'll be carrying when he comes is an MQ-1 Predator drone. We're supposed to have them, to use them. It's biblical."

His face was bounding around on his skull.

"Do you want me to try to set up a meeting with Peter and, of course, Angela?"

"Yeah."

Bruce turned to go.

"One more thing, while you're here, soldier. I'm getting a sneaking suspicion that someone on base is fucking with the drones."

"Why is that?" asked Bruce, his heart rate going up two ticks.

"I don't know. There've been a lot of crashes, especially of the Ravens, more than usual, more than I expected."

"Hardware?"

"Maybe. Probably. Panopticus is checking around with the mechanics."

"Could be design flaws back at Aero."

"I have to look at numbers, distribution. Could be software, too. In the trailers, satellite issues with command, who knows? But if there's someone fucking with the system, you can bet I'll get him. And the punishment will fit the crime, I can assure you."

He got up and attacked the curling bar.

"What would be appropriate?" Bruce inquired.

"Oh, I don't know. It depends. Destroying the cochlea, sucking out the pituitary, secret botox injections before trial." (Curl).

"How will you discover the criminal — if there is one?"

"These two eyes are all-seeing. (Curl). I've got my "sworn-never-to-lie-cheat-or-steal-or-tolerate-anyone-who-does" boys planted with their little cameras and recorders. They make lots of secret reports — regularly. And of course you know, Capt. Math, this place is bug and hack central. Lots of vulnerable devices: all computers and tablets, printers and routers, (curl), every communication to the cloud, ATM cards and gym lockers, (curl), your power strips and gaming consoles, (curl), your cars and smart thermostats, (curl), your medical devices, (curl), and every automobile communication. All information belongs to me. So we'll find him wherever he is if the limpdick prick exists." The curls continued.

"Oh, and one more answer to your personal question. I work out because, while I may not be the smartest or the tallest, or the most handsome in a room, I need to know that — push come to shove — I can kill anyone there."

The curls continued. Bruce and his autonomic nervous system left the gym with big time heebie-jeebies.

MIDLUDE IN HEAVEN

As we are reminded by the Rev. Gen. Creech, the first step on the noble Eightfold Path is Right View — right outlook or understanding on the way Reality works. A person with Right View understands why we exist, why we suffer, why there is greed and hatred among us. Right view will finally lead to self-awakening and liberation from the confines of samsara — the continual cycle of birth and death deriving from ignorance of the IS.

Escape from samsara is hard to come by in a civilization steered by 24-hour news cycles. But once one gets out of TV-range, beyond wi-fi and microwave, the IS begins to clarify. Such a place is Heaven (with a capital H). Maybe it's simple dispersion at the cube of the distance, maybe it's all those cumulous clouds blocking the signals, but up there (yes it is up, beyond terrestrial gravitas), they tend to know what's going on.

Such a knowledgeable gang was gathered in the poolroom, one smoking a black cigar. two drinking free beer, all taking turns at the pool table while watching the above events on a high-res screen above the bar.

So it is far from a mere authorial intrusion to report on their little shindig.

"To the four of them!" Cervantes lifted his glass in a toast to the screen."

"To the four," the rest said in chorus — all except the one with the cigar.

"To the four," he added, "in spite of themselves." And Brecht began to sing the song which had topped the heavenly charts last week — or was it last century? — in honor of the thousandth performance of *Mahagonny* down on earth. His voice was anything but heavenly.

>   *"Sie brauchen keinen Hurrikan,"* he sang.
>   *sie brauchen keinen Taifun.* Goethe joined in.
>   *denn was der an Schrecken tuen kann,*
>   *daß können sie selber, daß können sie selber, daß*
>   *können sie selber tun..."*

Mahler, showing off his English and impeccable rhythm, sang,

>   *"They do not need a hurricane*

They do not need a typhoon
For whatever horrors those can claim
They can do it themselves, they can do it them-
selves, they can do it themselves as soon…"

While Cervantes, not to be upstaged by the Germanics, added:

No necesitan el huracán
No necesitan el tifón
Porque todo lo qu'esos llevan
Lo hacen sí mismos, lo hacen sí mismos, lo hacen,
mi corazón.

The four marched around, toasting the quartet on the tube, splashing beer from their steins, making a helluva noise. Such seemed to be the considered view from heaven.

THE OTHER SHUES

While we're thus diverted from the plot, and speaking of songs, and in spite of Schubert's dominating the tale thus far, it behooves us to jump ahead to Robert Schumann who tilled the same fields of longing a few years later. The man was mad, of course, and ended his life (hmm — like Ravel…) in an asylum. But he was not so mad as to miss the sardonic opportunity to set a Heine poem in Brechtian contrast.

The text of *"Ein Jüngling liebt ein Mädchen"* is simple, but sad enough: A young man is in love with a girl who has chosen another. But this other loves yet another whom he marries. The spurned girl, in revenge, grabs the first man who comes along. Needless to say, the *Jüngling* is more miserable than ever.

Heine, overwhelmingly succinct, sums up the all the pain:

Es ist eine alte Geschichte
doch bleibt sie immer neu;
und wem sie just passieret,

dem bricht das Herz entzwei.

It's an old story, he says, but it remains ever new. And it breaks the hearts of those to whom it happens.

How much misery in that little phrase, *dem bricht das Herz entzwei.* The heart is broken in two. Not just broken, but broken in two.

And how does Herr Schumann set this song? Simple and sad? No — simple and antic, three verses in a boppy little ditty barely a minute long. Mean. Vicious.

Why do I bring this up? Because Peter and Bruce had actually played through the *Dichterliebe* one Wednesday evening when Angela showed up late. They got to *Ein Jüngling liebt ein Mädchen,* sang and played it through — and then went on to the next song about a shining, summer morning and forgiveness. What men don't talk about often looms over what they do.

And speaking of the unspoken, let us recall the first, and so far last, discussion among the four — the meeting and proposal to work on Ravel together.

The talk had been about music, but most thoughts were elsewhere — on Cybèle. All were charmed, of course. She was charming, *charmante* — her pert vivacity, her melodious accent, her sometimes exotic choice of words and grammar — so different from the trio's northeast origins, or the dry southwest it now inhabited. And she was beautiful, lovely. Angela could see that as well as the rest, and happily shared the sisterhood of grace.

Beyond that, Angela was proud of the work she had done with Cybèle over the weeks since her tattered arrival. Cybèle had opened up to tell her *"histoire"*, exposing the most sensitive wounds in a being long used to hiding them. She had been Angela's first real client — "friend" in Sekhmet-speak — but certainly counselee, and Angela being childless, the first deep relationship with a girl who could have been her daughter. Cybèle brought forth Angela's compassion, her perspicacity, her wisdom. Already, there was a bond between them. Angela understood that although she had been sexually violated so many times, Cybèle was still untouched, and truly belonged in Sekhmet's Maiden Room. She had presented Cybèle that night as her foundling, her friend, and her protégée. Cybèle, she thought. *Si belle.* What a perfect name.

Peter, like the others, found her charming, and his male eye thought her most attractive. He found himself subtly showing off in front of her, almost, if not quite, flirting. But foremost in his unthoughts was a sense, an intuition, of her freedom. He knew nothing of her story and her flights. He knew of nothing but her presence here, a tourist, away from home. But how different she seemed from *his* clients — and not just the obvious contrasts of gender, age, and life experience. Beyond her young beauty was a spirit which could never be contained in a cell, or even a SHU, the prison's Secure Housing Unit, the isolation facility for solitary punishment, protective custody, and potential suicides. Though unique in his experience, she was anything but solitary, The threads of her being seemed intimately intertwined with the air, the sunlight, the desert's space, and the far ocean's foam. She didn't need protection, he thought. Though her vulnerability might attract danger, he sensed it coupled with an even greater invulnerability which would guard her. He thought of the clotted faces of the men on his watch, the men in the SHU, and the men on the yard, or in his classes and groups. Though they all assumed cloaks of toughness, they were all tender inside. Most of them. A few not, but only a few. The reverse of Cybèle. The inside out of her. He thought of his own going "to prison" every morning. But these thoughts were continually scattered when swept and washed by her gentle current. She seemed a little bit of needed spice to life.

Bruce, too, was charmed, as who would not be? But his sub-musical thoughts initially concerned a theory concerning a golden ratio in facial beauty. Why was she so pretty, his tilted head wanted to know. He remembered a paper he had read in some government publication, NIH maybe, about the equations governing optimally attractive faces. The investigators used digitally manipulated photos of "good-looking" young women of all races, whose features they varied with respect to length, width, and distance between facial landmarks to assay optimum attractiveness to a mixed group of students. He thought he recalled that the Thurstonian attractiveness score varied regularly with some curvilinear function, but he couldn't remember the exact equation. The face's length minus its eye to mouth distance, divided by the eye to mouth distance...or something. He tried to derive it from her face, but she wouldn't hold still long enough. So he gave up. As for the others, her presence directed his latter thoughts to himself, to his own lack of attractiveness to the women he had courted, to his own theories explaining his effect on women and on the world in general. Aside from being exceedingly pretty, Cybèle was strong, if tiny, stuff.

While Peter and Angela, Bruce and Cybèle shared a discussion, mostly of poetry and music, their sub-surface thoughts were their own, each immured in his or her own, private SHU. Shoes protect, but they also crush the things beneath them.

Was this the *alte Geschichte*, the old story, always new? Not yet. It would take two Frenchmen to light the fuse.

CHANSONS MADECASSES

Between the first meeting of the four and the next, Cybèle had cut off her long chestnut hair. Why, oh why? Was she going through something gravely emotional? Perhaps. Did she simply want a cute, new look? Probably not. She was already cute enough for any observer, including herself. Was it a gesture of defiance, a quiet rebellion? Against whom?

Actually, it was a gesture of memory, a need to transform the bitter into the sweet, to do a good deed where a bad one had been done, to turn wrong into right, darkness into light. Alain had always loved her hair. He had incessantly extolled it, most memorably in the sunlight on the bridge at Place du Don where they had fastened their Cogex, their *cadena d'amour*.

Last week, in an issue of *Women's Health* at the guest house, Cybèle had seen an ad for Locks of Love. At first, she imagined the custom had now spread to America, that American lovers would now pledge their love on bridges instead of jumping off them. But then she found that Locks of Love had nothing to do with *cadenas* at all, but with hair. Hair Americans apparently called "locks". *Faux amis.* But these locks were to be donated to children who had lost their hair because of disease or cancer treatment, children too poor to afford wigs.

Why not? There was not much to do. They wanted more than ten inches. Hers was forty, and as they preferred, never bleached or permed. She often wore a ponytail or braid. And so, goodbye to Alain, and hello to…who- or whatever.

The other women at Sekhmet were ecstatic. Hers would be the nicest hair gift ever sent in institutional memory. Cybèle filled out an online form, and without a pang, but rather relief, sat down in a kitchen chair, and implored a sister to amputate. Angela watched the proceedings. Together, they bagged the braid in zip-lock, and sent it off in a large, padded envelope to some address in Florida. Her love, Angela's love, the collective love of the Sekhmet women went with it to whatever child or children would share in its glory.

Cybèle showed up for the first Ravel rehearsal in pixie cut.

Humbert Humbert might have called her

nymphic, if no longer a nymphette. Without her hair to distract, he would easily detect her limpid, fey grace, her shifty, soul-shattering, insidious charm. Her slenderness, her downy limbs were right up his obsessive alley. Yet if she seemed innocent — it was because she was. If there was coquetry in her behavior it was innocent coquetry, zestfulness, attractive fairyland élan.

Humbert would have known, too, that her name came from the greek *Kybele*, she of the hair, a Phrygian goddess of fertility. And would have appreciated the lesson that She Of The Hair became even more fetching as She Of The Pixie Cut.

And though Humbert Humbert was not at this first rehearsal, it was clear that all in the room were moved by the same admirations, intensified from before, but still latent.

They had their Ravel parts in hand.

"So what shall we try?" Peter asked.

Bruce responded from the piano. "Why don't we start with number one, and see how far we get?". Being punctilious, he liked to begin things at the beginning.

The *Chansons Madecasses* is a late masterwork written on commission for a specialized quartet (now modified with violin). Peter had remembered it when wondering what might fit the four of them. He had not remembered the music clearly or texts at all. When he had heard them, in childhood Cornell, he understood no French. I mention this to allay any suspicion that his choice was made for devious ends.

These three songs with their shocking texts had caused scandals even in Paris in the twenties with their explicit sexuality, and maddening inconsistency of view. Eroticism, exoticism, racial love and hatred made for an explosive combination even then, and ever since — especially this night, in this house, alone in the desert. And here's the funny thing: while the first and third song are overtly sexual, the words written from a male point of view, Ravel sets them for soprano. What does this mean? What is its effect?

The second song shockingly begins with the scream of a slave, Aoua!!, and demands that the listeners, most likely white, upper-class, be wary of white men, forked-tongue tyrants. The language is violent and male — carnage, vomiting, crushing, poison and death. The urgent message: *"Méfiez-vous des blancs"* — Do not trust the white man!

How odd then, how uncanny, in a way, to see and hear this waif-like young woman perform them in her native French, with her sylphlike charm, an angel with a touch of elf, seducing, denouncing, in strong mezzo-soprano.

Because of its musical difficulties and its emotional intensity, they could not do more than look at the first song that first rehearsal.

"*Nahandove*", is the most erotic of the three, specifically and explicitly erotic. *Nahandove, ô belle Nahandove!* The voice floats over the instruments at once narrating the sensuous setting and activity, and expressing the experience of the lover mating with his love on a bed of leaves and flowers. For Angela, given the singer and her appearance, there was more than a hint of lesbian ecstasy. For the men, well, the text functioned as one would think, even sung by a waif-like Cybèle. In expressing it, and in spite of herself, she embodied a demon, a Lilith, alluringly disguised as a female child.

Peter was overjoyed that for a good part of the piece, Ravel had left him alone with her, in cello and voice duet, with the other two merely watching. He was conscious that one of them was his wife, and he hid emotionally behind his sensitive playing, so full of subtle rubato, so engaged with the undulations of the vocal line.

When Bruce softly entered, it was a welcome intrusion, to announce the arrival of Nahandove. *Elle vient.* She comes. I recognize her breathing, the rustle of her skirt. It is she — *la belle Nahandove!* Peter couldn't stop himself from hearing "Cybèle-Nahandove. *Cybèle, la belle.* They played the duet together many times, and could finally engage with each other's breathing and hesitations.

And then arrived the snag that took up the entire evening — at least on its musical surface. All partook of the discussion and experimentation, though each had a unique slant. Here's the problem:

What is the climax of the text? That's right — climax. It's pretty clear. An adult knows a climax when he sees one. The the text says,

Tes baisers pénètrent jusqu'à l'âme;

tes caresses brûlent tous mes sens;

arrête, ou je vais mourir.

Meurt-on de volupté,

Nahandove, ô belle Nahandove?

Your kisses penetrate my soul, Your caresses burn all my senses. Stop or I will die. Can one die from ecstasy, Nahandove, oh lovely Nahandove?

Yup, it's the old love and death from the old in and out.

Surely, that's where the music, like the singer, and

players, male or female, must climax.

But no. Ravel carefully indicates the musical climax by a crescendo marked at its height by the *forte* entrance of the flute, now violin, on Nahandove's appearance. She is coming. I recognize the breathing of someone walking quickly; I hear the rustle of the skirt that enwraps her. It is she, it is she, it is she — the height of crescendo — *la belle Nahandove!* By the time of the poem's little death, the music is marked to be slower, and pianissimo. Not smoking a cigarette afterwards. During.

You see the problem. What to do? Follow the music, or follow the sense of the text? Psychoanalyze Ravel at a distance? The reader may not worry about such things, but musicians do. That's why they're musicians. Each of them came with a different understanding and approach.

The two who had a history of regular sexual congress overlapped somewhat in opinions, though hers was slightly different than his. The one who had never had a hit beyond first base (for him the hardest) had another. And the one for whom sex was twinned with horror had a fourth.

Bruce, an ordinal numbers guy, and a captain in the air force, wanted to obey the rules, and follow Gen. Ravel's instructions. Peter, based on civilian experience, thought the "come" passage should follow orders, but increase and decrease tempo. Poor Cybèle thought they should break the dynamic rules, and play more and more brazenly. And Angela, who ultimately prevailed — for what else could be done with such disagreement? — thought they should just trust their musicianship, listen to one another, listen to the music, listen to the text, and follow whatever was organically happening, perhaps different each time through.

But it took all evening, and much tempo, dynamic, and rhythmic experimentation to get there, and to be satisfied that there was no solution but attending presence. And even so, that hardly describes what was going on.

The men, in their very different ways, were in love. Peter had fallen into Ravel's trap, and was luxuriating in the sensuality of Cybèle's un-Nahandovian and so-Nahandovian allure. But, as they said in high school, "not just for her body". Clearly. Her body was too meager for that kind of thing. That meagerness enabled her fine, peculiar, soul to shine through more brightly. It was *shee with her beauty blazing* again, and again entwined with him in sensuous duet. But unlike with Angela, her blaze was less corporeal, more delicate. No prisoners would salivate with the thought of sticking themselves into that. And unlike with young Angela, he was now married.

So what? This was not serious. He understood that. She was only a kid. A little kid.

Bruce, on the other hand, was confronted at a new level with his unattractiveness. Peter was married, jealously married to Angela, so no competition there. He wasn't so much disturbed by the fucking as by thinking of Cybèle naked on a bed of leaves , blossoms and aromatic herbs. He had gone beyond the equations of her face to the semi-solid geometry of her body. the integrals of her curves, such as they were, and valleys. and he realized that in no way would his lines and angles lie comfortably upon them. Besides, his breath stank. And what would he do with his friend's assignment to show test-interest in his wife? How could he address two women at once, when even one had ever-eluded him?

But so what? This was not serious. He understood that. She was only a kid. A little kid.

Angela, too, was smitten. She knew Cybèle far better than the men. Cybèle could be her sister or her child. She could even be her first same-sex lover, should things come to that. But she knew her quickened heart was not serious. She understood that. Cybèle was only a kid. A little kid. Moreover, and foremost, Cybèle was her client.

Such was the state of affairs at the end of their first rehearsal.

Or was it?

Only a kid? Well, I suppose — comparatively. But:

UNDER THE SIGN OF THE SUBJUNCTIVE

Suddenly Peter had thought to himself, "Perhaps I have a second home, where everything I might do, like everything she does, is innocent."

He knew that one notices not every possibility along the road, but only those that call forth truth in one's own mind, truths that have only to be awakened to appear — so that one knows them already, and instantly.

But this thought was weighed down by lingering doubts of its decency. On the other hand, the feeling, the vague trill around such a boundary was not unpleasant.

He would like — perhaps later, in private — to say something to her about experiencing this, but with what words? It wasn't that he lacked the courage to do so, but how? How could she really understand? He would say something in French. He thought it might be easier, and later plausibly deniable if it came to that, the comical gropings around in a foreign language, yes, but mainly because such words would be marked for her alone, and not for any outsiders. For her alone, this inscrutable attention, and for others — silence. About this, this hidden path that might lead from one love to another, from first love to greater love.

What did Nietzsche say? Our sense of "morality" was like advising a tight-rope walker out over an abyss to just hold himself as stiffly as possible? Well, that's not great advice, especially for those of us with a well-understood sense of morality. Not so stiff, please.

Two people, like Cybèle and me, once we have found ourselves in such harmony, even over an abyss, well, we can maybe play a little game of hide and seek, our own *ricercare*, like Bach, a little hiddenness, a little deception, a little anarchy in love. What fun! Two small masks, both innocent.

But this image, playful, and a bit forced, like someone "being happy" instead of just being happy — especially when the game was so unknown and potentially dangerous — threw a kind of net over Peter's fantasy, and the images drooped and withered in his brain.

When he watched her leaving the house, her vocal score held lovingly against her breast, when he drank in that parting image of her so sublime, he had noted simultaneously his countermanding absence of will, a leeriness of being carried away into a danger zone, the image of the man on the yellow triangle being zapped by lightning, dancing perhaps his *Totentanz*. Very Mahler scherzo, jah, jah, and something froze within him. Was this for real? Did he really want her?

In the floating quandary he flashed on a memory of a still-unforgettable girl at one of his father's faculty concerts. She was there with her parents, people he didn't know, had never seen, sitting in the row in front of him, two seats to his right so he could see her hair, her neck, her profile, his own age she was, or a little younger, and he twelve, thirteen and he didn't hear a note all night, so in love was he. He followed the family out at intermission, and studied her carefully. For the second half of the concert he was twice as smitten. He and his mom had to meet his father in the green room, so while his beloved walked up the stairs after the applause, he had to walk the other way down them. And now she was only a bygone love poem, the bliss gone, the flaming infatuation, and — mysteriously — never to be repeated. This event he had always hidden from Angela, and only now he felt guilty over it.

How would she have treated him, she, his pre-teen love? Beautifully, tenderly, like the perfection she seemed? With total charm no doubt, the harp in the Adagietto.

The tense, high wire walk of the once-and-never-again. How wonderful it would be to transcend all limits.

But he already had too much adult trouble to re-engage the disarming seriousness he had as a child. He was left with only an formless, shape-shifting hunger, sometimes animal, sometimes human. A promise of rescue — but from what? Fermata. GP. Real life began to reign.

But if not now, when?

More Subjective: Passion In The Desert: Bruce In Love.

Bruce took counsel with himself.

Initially, it seemed so natural, so easy, so simple, so obvious to declare his love, maybe making fun of his own cloddishness, naiveté, whatever, inviting her to laugh at him because look how silly he was, crying inside and laughing, the sun peeking out from the dark clouds of Bruce.

Yes, she had unwittingly mined it, that thing buried deep in his heart, at the S-A node perhaps, that thing to which he would never admit or confess even under hazing, even under torture, as if it were a treasure chest anchoring his unimpeachable rightness, erected carefully with the tools of logic in the forests of chaos. That rightness was his one fortress, his *feste Burg* against the onslaughts of human perfidy.

Now what? Could he actually betray himself down to the foundations? It was enough to make all shift, and modulate into bizarre and unfamiliar keys. But the damage, the deed was done. His unimpeachability impeached. Another treasure had been revealed, but what else might be lurking down there at the bottom of the Rhine? A — the ultimate — Rhinemaiden?

What he had always imagined to be impenetrable armor suddenly struck him as charming — Woody Allen defenses, same glasses, same blinking eyes, an illuminating re-interpretation of his strategy against an overpowering wash of life. It was not bad, it was not good, there was no + or - here, no vector into space or into others, it was not fitted to impale anyone. What, after all, had she said to him that addressed anything except Ravel? Nothing. And yet that nothing was battering against him, knifing into him, stabbing at his poor Woody Allen head, you shouldn't hit a man with glasses, and now there was blood, a crown of thorns, even passion in the desert of his life. Great disorder reigned. Best to freeze, to hold himself stiff. He couldn't endure even the smallest attack of feeling. He would collapse, disintegrate, and fragments would fly — soggy, misshapen, immense, explosive ecstasy. Anaphylaxis. He hated her, hated her cruelty.

On the other hand, he feared nothing more than becoming rational again.

Breathe deeply, Bruce. As if to attack the *Appasionata*. Yes, breathe deeply, Bruce.

He took another tour inside himself.

1 The world is all that is the case.

1.1 The world is the totality of facts, not of things.

1.11 The world is determined by the facts, and by their being all the facts.

1.12 For the totality of facts determines what is the case, and also whatever is not the case.

1.13 The facts in logical space are the world.

He felt…nothing. Only a small lump above his diaphragm, a sensation some child might feel after a good cry. Or in his case, a manikin, for he was not a child.

He had learned no lesson, but he was aware that something inside had shifted.

On his way back to Creech which, with its stark ranks of one-story concrete barracks and chain-link fences, looked more like a minimum-security prison than his home, he gradually deadened and filmed over, back into his usual acuteness.

She thought: Love between people of the so-called same sex is really nothing different than love between people of different sexes. It's just the usual commandment to love thy neighbor — even without knowing what kind of person she may be. A test, perhaps, of the iffy relationship between love and reality.

It occurred to Angela that she too, like everything and everyone else, lived a basically passive life, a captive in her own being, committed to a place, a husband, a work life, a habitation, playing out only one possibility of herself year after year. That Angela-being was admittedly a good one, happy enough, and yet she found herself full of new, incomprehensible urges to become another.

Almost mournfully, she considered splitting, leaving the desert, the possible dark delight of being unfaithful to her habitation. All her clinging, her almost anxious clinging to Peter and Peter's world, quietly called itself out as being — could it be? — completely arbitrary, maybe even superficial — compared with the barely grasped possibilities of the utterly other.

She saw everything she was doing in the light of surrender, not the good surrender to the goddess, but as something like self-impaling self-subjugation, the abandonment of her real being, her Self, leaving her with only the shell of her beautiful, but mere, appearance.

She wasn't trying to be audacious — nothing like that — but she felt almost reproachful at the small-B-being she was, and that little ache became a larger pain when she thought she might deserve nothing better. Look at the other women who flowed through Sekhmet. Seekers, yes, but only because so needy. And what did *she* really need, other than what she had?

She *could* love someone else. She could probably be married to *anyone* — provided she loved him — or her — in the first place.

Wearing The Sign Of Sin

The desert night was unbearably lovely, the warm breeze caressing. And yet, as Peter drove her back to Sekhmet, with the top down, Cybèle suddenly felt inside her a pianissimo scream, a wispy cloud scream, a soap bubble scream, which barely moved from her chest to her throat, tasting, just the slightest, a *soupçon*, of lust. She wanted out of the car, but that was silly. Yet she did want out — *un peu* — from all this, this new music, these Évariste texts, these new friends. *Ils sont doux, oui, mais peut-être trop.* She felt her sweet face become hideous, and flit around inside her skull. Her hands went to her breasts, and she inhaled deeply. The desert air was chaste. OK. OK. *C'est encore normal.*

In order to die, she thought, you need only to be alive.

And though she be but little, she was fierce.

The Madman Comes To Visit

Bruce kept his promise to bring the Rev. General Madman to visit with Peter and Angela. The General satisfied his lecherous agenda by so going. After a few drinks, and some not-so-subtle ogling the talk began to open up among institutions.

"Tell me more about Secmet," their guest inquired. "Is that a code name for something? Security something? "

"How do you know about us?" Angela asked. "Have you visited the Temple?" Hmm. She had a sexy voice, too.

"No. I've seen your folks out on the road in front of the gate."

"Did you hear what they were chanting?"

"No, no. I just saw the video. And you can never really know if the words on signs actually mean what they say, first order. In spy land, we live in a world of free-floating signifiers." This was well-rehearsed, and, besides his open shirt on hairy 52" chest, was meant to impress her. Her husband struck him as being of possibly sound mind but insufficient body. At least for a bod like hers.

Angela responded: "Sekhmet was the lion-headed goddess of war and destruction…"

"Really? That's great! Wonderful to have you in the neighborhood! I'd thought maybe you were a bunch of goddam harpy peaceniks. Excuse the language."

"The sun god created her Sekhmet as a weapon of revenge to destroy men for their wicked ways," Peter put in.

"Exactly, exactly. That's what we do. The best answer to bad guys with guns is good guys with drones. Coming right out of the sky like sunlight."

"So humanity developed elaborate rituals hoping Sekhmet could be appeased," Angela elaborated. "Temples with more than 700 statues of the goddess." Bruce was having a ball watching all this.

"You have 700 statues out there at your place?"

"Seven hundred is an average among temples. A mean, actually," Bruce noted.

"No," Angela picked up, "we have only one. She sat at the southern wall, facing the Nevada Test Site.'"

"Sat? Why sat? What did she, mosey over to the Test Site for supper?"

"She was missing the other day. Someone stole her."

"How big was she?"

"Oh, about four feet tall, sitting on a throne.

"Weigh a lot?"

"I'd guess a few hundred pounds at least. We saw tire tracks in the sand outside.

"Was she black? I mean, is she black?"

"Yes. How did you know?"

"I think I saw her at the base. Stashed in Storage C. I was going to ask the grounds crew about her. You think she's after us? We're the good guys."

"I'd say she was stolen," Peter offered.

"Why would anybody do that?"

"A problem with women? Women goddess? Someone who wasn't happy with a temple dedicated to women?" Angela proposed.

"Hey, our guys love women. Love 'em up a storm. Can't get enough of 'em. Some of them are married…"

"Captain Boynton wondered if we had seen the Sun article last week about violence against women in the military, and the incident over at the base," Peter let on.

"And of course we had," Angela confirmed. "It's an issue we share, Peter and I, in our workplaces."

"I can't talk about it. Ongoing investigation. Security."

"Of course," Peter said. "But it is an issue, right? In military units?"

"Oh yeah, sure. Men without women, you know. Like frogs without a pond."

"That's of course our situation at the prison. Bruce told you I was an assistant warden over there?" Creech nodded. "Sometimes it gets confusing what with my last name."

"Warden Warden. Good one."

"Like Major Major," said Bruce. If the base commander got the reference, he didn't seem to want to discuss it.

"I mean it's pretty wide-spread, right?" Peter continued. "Probably less at Creech, where many of the men drive home at night — the most dangerous part of their day — but in more isolated places? I think there were something like 20,000 sexual assaults cross services last year?"

"Yeah, well, a lot of women just say that…"

"And that's only the ones reported," Bruce observed.

"Well, it is a problem," Creech admitted. "Somewhat of a problem. Pedictable. We've planned for it."

"Oh, good." Peter remarked. "How?"

"How what?"

"How do you plan for it? I ask because we obviously have similar problems at HDSP."

"I mean we expect it," the general explained.

"And what do you do about it?" Angela asked.

"We're...we've appointed a study committee — with a woman on it. They haven't come up with any recommendations, yet."

"We were thinking, Bruce and Angela and I, about whether we might do some project together, the three of us. The prison and Creech and the Temple. Something that would get our men thinking about their behaviors toward women, maybe changing them." Peter was improvising. They had not talked about it together. But the others let him riff. "I mean, many, probably most of our men, aside from other things, have violence against women on their rap sheets. Wives, girlfriends beaten. Domestic violence."

"I'll bet," Madman said, "But ours is not so widespread..."

Bruce disagreed. "I don't know. In basic training, we had to chant some pretty nasty things about women, which I won't repeat here. Both to establish our togetherness-manhood, and when we lashed out at targets. With bayonets."

"Yeah, well, that doesn't really mean..."

"OK, OK," Peter said. "The point is could we come up with a program — we could share expenses, share space — that would speak to your guys and ours?

"It'd have to have music to get through to ours," Creech said. "They're plugged in, 24/7."

"Even when they're pushing the kill buttons?" Angela asked, aghast.

"Sure. That's when they need it most. Rhythm, verve. I think they listen to rap to get them in the mood."

"Music. Very good idea," said Bruce. "I think we can handle that."

"You two play music, too?" Peter and Angela nodded. "What do you play?"

"He plays cello, I play violin."

"Oh. Classy. I bet you make beautiful music together."

"They play together with me," Bruce said. "We have a trio."

"Great. Like piano, bass and drums?"

"Kind of," Bruce said.

"Yeah, I love that stuff."

They agreed on a joint project using music. The Air Base, the prison, and Sekhmet, too. The musicians would think about just what and how.

The rest of the evening went well. While Peter & Angela had some background on Creech via Bruce, the general was most curious about what went on in the prison. Peter described the tensions between the warehouse guys and the rehabilitation guys, how new PC freedoms could wind up placing staff at risk, but did we want to go back to the old days of prison as retribution, punishment. He was in charge of developing a more progressive model, and described the ed component, the therapy groups, the writing, poetry, and theater workshops."

"So those men don't wind up right back in the joint?"

"Fewer. Half as many."

"I'd rather we keep them off the streets," the general said.

"I'd rather we put them back on the streets," said Angela, "but less violent, more productive. We're all human, you know."

"Yes, ma'am. But some are more human than others. Some of our guys don't seem very human to me. When there's a kill, everyone in the trailer whoops and cheers. Not them. The less-than-humans just sit there. Like robots. No team spirit."

"You think your women feel on the same team, when they always have to be wary of sexual assault."

"Whoa!" Creech objected ."Not all women. Not always."

"Yes, all women, and yes, always." Beauty — and anger — blazing.

The general shrugged it off, and changed the topic. Strategic retreat. If they were going to work or play together, he didn't want a fight so soon. But she was a feisty one. Hot damn!

FROG POND

After the testosterone bath, Peter and Angela needed a breath of fresh air. It was August — summer thunderstorm season in an El Niño year— and a week ago it had poured down an inch and a half in two hours, and the kwaah-kwaah-kwaahs were fiercely singing their kwaah-kwaah-kwaah passion. ""kwaah-kwaah-kwaah, kwaah-kwaah-kwaah", audible even in the house.

I should say a word about the frog pond and the frogs. In this case, the frogs were not frogs, but toads, and unlike men without women, they did have a pond, at least a temporary one. Peter and Angela thought of this occasional amenity as the pool at the Estivation Hotel, an Econolodge designed for and exclusively occupied by western spade foot toads, *Spea hammondii*, with two "i"s, a species that normally covers itself in slime, digs holes, and buries itself under the summer desert floor. Sleeping vegetables. When it rains, they surface, sing madly, and do their animal thing.

They lay their eggs in post-deluge ponds, not much more than puddles. The tadpoles grow up fast. They had better, or fried tadpole is their collective fate. In two weeks or less they are adults, practicing cannibalism along the way — to speed their growth with congeneric protein. When the puddle pool dries out, the few survivors use their spades to dig anew, and like mom and dad, resume estivation.

If the next rains come in time, the sonorous cycle is repeated. If not, that particular colony will, like little desert mermaids, become foam on the sea of sand, dust in the wind. Like Peter's father.

Clearly they are singing, and not just signaling or talking. Choruses of tricky counterpoint, sections of alto, tenor, bass. With each croak their throats bubble out and collapse, all through the night. Facing outward from the water, a toads-width apart, clanking and croaking a timeless dirge nowhere near jubilant. Why? What are they dirging about? Love, no doubt, since that is their chief current business. Coolness? Wetness? Courage? An acknowledgement of the common life?

And their song, of course, attracts their predators — snakes, coyotes, owls. And so love is once again sutured to death, and the survivors of the sun will likely not survive its children.

Peter and Angela held hands as they stood there, musicians listening carefully, and in wonder. But though their fingers were joined, their hearts were not one. Each was absent, engaged with an invisible other, and that other was the same for both.

Four Part Invention

Absence makes the heart grow fonder, and in Peter's case "fonder" meant both greater love, and growing folly. And even "absence" was bivalent. On the one hand his new crush was almost always eight miles distant — at Sekhmet — and with his wife and others there, he couldn't very well sneak out of his life to see her. It drove him bats, and fonder. On the other hand, he missed his wife, who no longer monopolized his heart. He missed his marriage, and their old, exclusive love. He missed the exclusivist jealousy which had led to a mad proposal to Bruce. And with these absences, his love for Angela intensified. To watch her preparing a meal seemed nothing less than watching a goddess play ping pong, so much did he still adore. His lust for a bugging device became simply a lover's need to hear her every word, her every sigh.

And yet, Cybèle, Cybèle, la belle Cybèle!!

Yes, a great many problems in their relationship

had become buried under the structures of his married life, and his current confusion left him no room to uncover them, and work them out. Or even to imagine things different than they had become. Cybèle had entered their lives like a living signpost indicating other roads, excavation ahead, shoveling out like a spadefoot toad. Yet Peter stood paralyzed, as the sun beat down and the season changed beneath him. He knew he could not repair everything, and least of all, the rent he had torn in their fabric. But he could at least not ruin things. He would sit down with Angela and confess, tell all, ask for understanding — and forgiveness. And he knew, even as he thought it, that asking for understanding and forgiveness was really asking for permission. He would speak with her that night.

—◦◦◦—

With Bruce, absence made the man to ponder. But it was like an equation with three unknowns. Four, if he counted his assignment as Angela's tempter. He had cancelled her out of the equation because though she was beautiful, and brilliant, and a great musician, and sexy as hell, she was his, Peter's, she was his wife, till death do them part, he supposed, though he couldn't remember Schubert contracting for that at the service. Angela was his friend, in the guise of a delightful woman, though that, of course, complicated things as always.

But with Cybèle, it was otherwise. Decidedly. She belonged to no one. She needed someone. Could that someone be he? The zhlub and the fairy? Woody comes a-courting? Froggy and nifty Miss Mousy? He didn't think that story ended happily.

And then the absence of her. He never saw her except at rehearsals. Angela saw her every day, but she didn't desire her. Peter saw her now and then, and he was married. But he, he, the eligible party, when did he ever see her alone? Maybe he'd invite her to work on some lieder with him. Mahler. Even French folk songs. They're not bad. But where would they meet? The piano at the Baptist Church would be an insult, and would hardly show off his art. The piano at the base was little better, and in a raucous bar full of drooling military goons. The only good piano, the only good, romantic setting, was chez Warden where they would certainly be detected. This was a far more difficult problem than devising canzicrans to bring down drones.

Had he flaunted his Ravel knowledge at her, his impeccable technique — to ease his embarrassment?

212

Flaunting — she wouldn't like that. It wouldn't have been hard to do. Yes, she had brains and beauty in that little head, but she was innocent and trusting, probably no better educated than a little animal. She didn't seem to look behind anything; she appeared only to see the thing itself. Still, he felt as one with her. Magically. It's not as if he saw himself in her or she in him. Far from it. Or that she was really his own secret self disguised behind her stranger eyes. They had little enough in common. But he felt an absolutely unbreakable and deeply necessary connection, some materialization of their opposites. He was no less attracted than alarmed.

But he was readying himself for an adventure he had never had before. He needed only the courage to set out. He felt he was alive — with a brand-new beating heart. He had to yield to his emotion, even should that be un-Bruce-like. But it must be right, a symptom his larger righteous war against reality: love scaling a loveless world. He had discovered the core of all his criticism — Love. He so loved the world that he would give his newly-begotten self up to its seduction. Despite everything, incrementally, very gently, he would find an approach to Cybèle, penetrate that armor of vivacity, and perhaps Love and a new life would smile upon him.

How Bruce made it from Sunday night to Wednesday evening, how that impassioned noodle, steeped and saturated in love, found the strength to endure an infinitely divisible time span, is truly something to be praised.

—⁓—

For Angela, presence broke the heart asunder. Cybèle's presence — at Sekhmet, and now in Peter's life, and her own, had stretched her heart in ways she hadn't experienced since Berkelely. And Peter hadn't even confessed to her yet — as if a wife needs a confession to know when something strange is going on. They had had so much to talk over about their marriage, their current life when a child came into their worlds, an eighteen-year old, far younger than she. She felt degraded, helpless at losing out because of being born seventeen years too soon.

She understood — at least she thought she understood — that she was still the greatest event in Peter's life, that when they were together, especially making music, that their souls spiraled upward, entwined, and their sense of contact was so strong as to be inexpressible. Then they had to find impersonal things to talk about.

But the wrench in the works, the twisted blade in the heart, was that she, too, was falling in love with Peter's beloved. His second beloved. All she had suffered as a pampered California teenager had sunk into oblivion when she met the man who was now her husband. But now, that tranquility and seclusion had been shattered. She tried to remember those couple-only days, but they wafted into her memory like late-afternoon in a room in which windows had too-long been closed.

And yet, Cybèle, Cybèle, la belle Cybèle, her sister-wife!! She felt helpless in the complexity of all this. She understood what was going on inside her as little as does a woman growing a child in her womb. It lay beyond the reach of words, of music, and could not be expressed by any action. Whatever it was, it simply had to be embraced, explored, patiently awaited in a cloak of silence. To abide the stirrings of two passionate beings, there was only one approach: rigorous, constant planning.

For Cybèle, presence made the heart much sounder. Angela's presence in her life. Sekhmet's presence, repairing the wounds inflicted by her frères, reversing a logic of male domination, helping her to express her feelings, to explore her emotional understanding. She was healing! The cutting of her flybait hair, so over-capable of attracting male insects — what a weight lifted from her shoulders, physically and psychologically, what an inspired act. Sekhmet-inspired, goddess-inspired, Angela-inspired. Yet still a gift to some hurting child.

And the rehearsals. How wonderful to accepted as a peer by real musicians, to actually sing that piece, to scream out *Aoua!* against enslavement, *Méfiez-vous des blancs, des garçons blancs*, to imagine lying down with her violin love on a bed of leaves and herbs and flowers in suggestive love play, a floating duet of souls.

A young woman tells herself she is in love for the first time, and now truly inhabits the world of grownups. She might have had crushes before, yet the moment comes when she tells herself she is truly in love and all her thoughts take on something of oaf-ishly sensual affection. When she stood singing near her love's music stand, she felt a fraud, masquerading in her compact physical appearance, while actually being a haphazard roil of emotions encased in a picture-book husk. In a way it was sad, but she was happy. It was all by chance, a dream become real-ity. She imagined everything that would happen, her own gestures of ecstatic surrender, her flowering in Angela's bosom. Her daughter, her sister, her lover.

—⁓—

There was a curious little coda to this four part invention, in no way wagging the dog of the tale. After leaving the Warden's that night, driving his jeep back to the base, the Rev. Gen. Madman Creech III reflected at length on his dead black lab, the one true love of his life, the only being who never wanted more from him than love to be returned.

En Attendant Javert: Notes In The Captain's Mailbox

432ND WING ☀ United States Air Force ☀
Creech Air Force Base

2/13/10

We at 432 have a drive to explore the unknown
and to be a part of a bigger thing. The only
law that really matters is the Law of 9/11.

432ND WING ☀ United States Air Force ☀
Creech Air Force Base

2/17/10

If I were you, I would understand clearly
the concept of "double taps". These, of
course, are follow-up strikes on those who
arrive to help (enemy) victims. We understand that double tap strikes on responders
violate international law. To this objec-
tion, I answer, "So?"

432ND WING ☀ United States Air Force ☀

Creech Air Force Base

2/22/10

We drone warriors are clearly unlawful combatants, invisible fighters without uniforms, employing armed force contrary to the laws and customs of war. We embrace unlawful combat against any enemy, foreign *or* domestic. We intend to win our battles.

432ND WING ☀ United States Air Force ☀

Creech Air Force Base

3/2/10

You once inquired where the term "bug splat" originated. In 2003, the Department of Defense developed a computer program designed to give operators a better sense of the human toll of a particular attack. In it, the dead show up as blob-like images resembling squashed insects. QED. The program was subsequently named "BUG SPLAT". I am smelling BS in the air.

432ND WING ☀ United States Air Force ☀

Creech Air Force Base

3/9/10

THE AIRMAN'S CREED:

I am an American Airman.
I am a Warrior.
I have answered my Nation's call.
I am an American Airman.

I am faithful to a Proud Heritage,
A Tradition of Honor,
And a Legacy of Valor.
I am an American Airman.
Guardian of Freedom and Justice,
My Nation's Sword and Shield.
I defend my Country with my Life.
I am an American Airman.
I will never falter,
And I will not fail.

Ominous.

But the Captain, as was his way, kept these tidings to himself. Or perhaps he was considering the sign hanging over Madman Creech's desk: EVERY MASTER EMBRACES HIS OWN DEATH.

ANATOMIES

In April, shortly after the event we know had occured, the remnant three discussed the possibility of a memorial service for Bruce's birthday in September. They were musicians. They could play music.

But what? The symbolism should be obvious. (Musicians love symbolic gesture.) A piece for piano, voice, violin and cello — without the piano. Touching. O-Captain-my-Captainish. What piece, then? A mass — shrunken by the multitude that was Bruce.

His favorite mass? Not the B minor, not the Missa Solemnis, not the Brahms Requiem — but that little Schubert Mass in G, the easy one, the one all church choirs could sing, even his. They had all played or sung it before.

Agnus Dei, qui tollis pecatta mundi, dona nobis pacem. Sure. That lovely movement. They were all sinners; they could all use peace. Including the departed.

(Which leads one to wonder: Why, in the story of

this quartet, none centered in song, per se, is Schubert the master who arises most frequently — in a coming-together, a courtship, a wedding, a dream, and now a departing benediction?

Musicians have their hierarchies, personal and traditional. (Musicians love hierarchies.) The tradition, one, shared by all in the west, is worship for "the three Bs — Bach, Beethoven, and Brahms — a religion well-founded.

The great anatomizers of human body, mind and spirt, of individual, group, and universe — though which was the greatest explorer of each is debated. In any case, they divide the possibilities among them.

But Schubert begins with an S. Or as Cyrillics think, with a Ш. But not a B. What is he doing here, upstaging the usual gang? Could it be that Schubert, initial aside, suggests another basic element beyond the traditional triads? A fourth voice in the Great Harmony? Body, mind, spirit. Individual, group, cosmos. What is left? Line up the usual suspect.

It's Love — love, love, Love. The All-You-Need-Is kind. Not Bruce-love. Not lust-love. Not even Romeo-and-Juliet-love love. But *caritas*, the binder of souls, of world, of universe. Among them, could Bruce — with his kyphotic back and coke-bottle glasses — could Bruce have been the source of S, the font of Ш, the

inner accompanist, the unnoticed uniter of all things
great and small? An odd thought.)

They discussed a memorial service, but, after all,
who would come? The idea was dropped, never to
rise again.

But with this speculation, we jump the gun, half-
cocked.

A Child Is Made

Peter was already in bed, reading *À la recherche du temps perdu*. He had just finished *Du côté de chez Swann*, and was now starting *À l'ombre des jeunes filles en fleurs*. Since the arrival of Angela's client and protégée, the trio's new colleague and friend, and also, of course, their work on *Chansons madecasses*, he had decided to work on his French. He loved those old Gallimard editions with their tan and red covers, their elegant red and black fonts. Back in college he had loved cutting the pages when they were new, and Proust was one of the few bookish things the Wardens had lugged around with them in the course of his career travels. Now, at last, the set had been unpacked for permanent residence, display, and reminder of the Berkeley days, looking and smelling better than ever as the paper aged and yellowed as it had in nineteenth century France. The reflective bedroom skylight had already cleared, and the stars blazed above him from the late September sky.

When Angela came in, he put down his book, and watched her undress, an always — and still, even in the present muddy — a most pleasing moment in his day. But tonight was to be a different night, long-planned, but not over-rehearsed or completely determined.

"I've gotten to like your tramp stamp" he said, opening with the old, perhaps worn, say-something-vaguely-but-not-explicitly-sexual gambit.

"Oh, yeah?" she responded. "Took you long enough," (not an auspicious response), picked up her book from her bed table, and switched on her reading light. What was she reading? *El ingenioso hidalgo don Quijote de la Mancha*. Having moved to the southwest, and for other closer reasons, she had decided to work on her Spanish with Cervantes and her Nook.

"How's the Don doing with Dulcinea?"

"Haven't gotten to her yet. The Don say's she's terrific, beyond rational reflection."

"I can't wait to meet her."

There was a grand pause with a fermata. Five seconds of silence trying to decide whether it was an uncomfortable, or simply two animals settling their nests, the start of some mutual reading.

"Sweetie?" Peter hesitated.

"What?"

"We have to have talk."

"Hm. OK. About what?" As if she didn't suspect.

"I've fallen in love with Cybèle." Good old, blunt Peter, getting to the point. Angela put down her Nook and turned over to face him.

"You're not mad?" he inquired.

"No, of course not. Everybody is in love with her. Bruce is in love with her. Even I'm in love with her a little. Why shouldn't you be? She's very lovable. We all love her at the Temple."

"But I think it's getting in the way of our relationship."

"Are you fucking her?" Blunt Angela getting to the point.

Peter, shocked: "No, no, of course not. She's always with you or at the Temple."

"The Temple is not a prison. I don't see her all the time. And who knows where you go when you go 'to work' or 'stay late for a meeting'."

"I told you…"

"Yes, yes, you're not fucking her. But you'd like to."

"No…I mean, sure, but — as you say, everyone would. I mean she's sexually attractive in a waif-like way. Half-pixie, half…"

"Half what? Half-whore?"

"No, no, what are you talking about? She's the last girl on earth you…"

226

"Half-kitten? Half-swallow?"

Peter was getting angry. This was not going as planned. Angela, surprised, was having a strange kind of fun she'd never had with him, teasing, exploring, engaging her anxiety and resentment but in a non-apocalyptic way. She too had been concerned with a three-body problem — as Bruce would say — an equation with three unknowns. She was angry at Peter for being such a predictable male, angry at herself for being angry at him while duplicating his emotional infidelity. Confusing. Confused. She reached out to touch his bare shoulder. Cool hand, he thought. Her bow hand. Strong.

He placed his left hand on her right, and they both took a breath together as they had so many times in duet.

"I'm glad you told me," she said, *piano*, *grazioso*. "I'm open to talking more about it."

While her apparent forgiveness was liberating, it didn't solve many complications. It did, however, result in a natural hug between them, a long hug, longer than most. And long hugs between healthy, handsome people, scantily clad in bed on a cool, late summer night tend to develop much like a Beethoven sonata: a slow introduction in uncertain keys followed by an accelerando, or, alternatively, right-bang into an allegro appassionato which develops, eases, and returns to its beginning — changed — a familiar sonata, many times played between them.

By the time their glances met, the decision had been made and all prohibitions were now behind them. Their understanding announced itself with every breath. She, who had been deserted by her desire for her husband, now seized his hand. And yet she was briefly bewildered by this skin and bone piece-of-strange-person she held tightly to her breast.

Peter's mind was not yet blank. He was pondering what it might be like to be really — literally — attached to his wife. Who knows what such a diploid nervous system might become, united not only by a single bloodstream, but by the very effect of total interdependence? Would his every sensory or emotional twinge be felt, too, by Angela, and in the same way even though it was experienced in her body, not his? Would they experience music identically? And if Angela ever fell in love elsewhere, would he then love her lover, too?

He told himself not to be afraid. The darkness they embraced in was no deeper than the darkness inside his own body — which did not frighten. Two darknesses separated by a thin layer of skin.

As he came toward climax, he thought perhaps

they might be heading for some unimaginable sorrow in love, worse than Schubert, worse than Schumann, worse than Mahler, and almost longed to pull out, to apologize, to turn away. With great effort, he pushed up over her, while still remaining inside.

"Are you ok?"

"Oh, sweetie, yes…"

Man, *homo loquens,* the only beast that pursues conversation even during reproduction, the attending bliss tightly bound to the loquacity that spawned the notion of God as "logos". Introduction, allegro, return, and sometimes a little coda, an envoi to what just happened, a gentle fare-thee-well. In this particular case, it was not so gentle:

"Hey! Did you come?"

"What do you think?" Peter said sweetly.

"I mean did you come in me?"

"I guess so."

He had, he knew, launched a barrage of hemidemisemiquavers along her internal staff, aiming at the whole note they sensed below them. That's what he thought at the time, when thinking made its return.

"You came in me without a condom?"

"Yeah, well, it was a surprise visit."

"Jesus, are you nuts? You ready for a kid? Are we ready for a kid?"

"You're almost fifty years old."

"Yeah? Well, fifty is the new thirty-five. Have I mentioned anything to you about a change of life?"

"Don't be silly," Peter objected, though silliness was not in her repertoire. "We have a lot of flaky women in the women's unit, and no one over forty has ever come in pregnant. You know, the docs call any woman over 34 an elderly primigravida? What are the chances of Angela Warden being an elderly primigravida?"

"Grave, that's what — given the gods of irony and Murphy's Law. You don't think pre-menopausal women can have children?"

She stormed out of their excellently appointed bedroom to their excellently appointed bathroom to wash out with her father's thoughtful gift, rare in Nevada, a high-end, low-flow, Kohler bidet.

But she didn't storm out fast enough for those allegro 64th notes. After missing a second period, she home-tested positive for pregnancy.

A word here about water — bidet and otherwise — at the Warden House.

The Mojave is arid, but not bone-dry. I've described earlier the relatively lush conditions only eighteen miles southwest up Cold Creek Road. And there is a creek in Cold Creek. And the creek ran downhill toward the Wardens. And that single Joshua tree which had Robert Johansson jumping up and down, paying McKinney & Sons big bucks to drill down 435 feet to discover a small water-storage cavern, that single tree was also a signal which led to — among other things — a functioning bidet.

This represents a minor miracle. This location, this house in the middle of the desert, a nothing in a nowhere. Yet open a faucet, or push the bidet wash button — and water comes out. Electricity and gas are easy to imagine, but water! Water where no water is! How did it get here? It even tastes like water. You can drink your fill, slake your thirst. Somewhat staggering. Water may be the most surprising thing in the world, transparent, odorless, potable. What drips down your chin is already a marvel. And if you dive in, it separates around you instead of breaking your neck.

Yes, the house was designed for maximum water efficiency — with Clivus Composting Toilet and all that. But chez Warden was practically a breeder reactor for water. In fact, it *was* a breeder reactor, creating water out of thin air by means of a Whisson windmill. Look it up. An array of solar panels circulates a refrigerant to cool the blades of a specially designed windmill. Water from wind condenses on the blades, and is collected and stored. The Warden solar array also drove a pump to bring up water from the cavern. Between the two, pump and Whisson — if every drop is efficiently recycled, as it was — and if the normal drought conditions were not off the charts, there was more than enough water for two-person use. The bidet stream may have been a little low that night, but I suspect that Angela's was the correct guess. She was, in fact, preggers.

The Jig Was Up

I mean, if you think living with guilt and suspicion is hard, try living with guilt and knowledge.

As a gesture — perfectly appropriate — Peter would call off the spying on Angela. Whether she was seeing other men or not, and probably not, Peter was just not up for any test results.

Bruce would be immensely relieved. He needed to devote himself with mathematical precision to his terrorist mischief. And to also being in love with Cybèle.

Angela was unquietly weirded out and antsy. The quartet was suffering, and Ravel had missed the last two Wednesdays for rehearsal. Rehearsal for what, anyway?

The Truth Will Out. Honesty Is The Best Policy

Peter loved Angela still, but he was "in love" with Cybèle. It was love at first sight, he thought. Much has been said and written about love at first sight, and Love does have a tendency toward mythification. He knew this, of course. But he felt that his first sight of Cybèle was a bit of clairvoyance, sensing, intuiting, capturing the essence of her being, or rather of what her being would come to be for him. She had revealed herself to him the way some others discover God.

It wasn't that she was "his other half". You know — the Platonic tale of the gods dividing the spherical human original into halves, and these pathetic hemispheres spending their lives trying to find their amputations? Peter loved stories as well as the next, but he understood, both theoretically and empirically, why "my other half" was nonsense (and this is why he was a likely buddy for Bruce). No one can know which of the other amputees is his own missing part.

They grab anyone that seems right, they graft themselves to one another, and the transplant is likely to be immunologically rejected. And if a child is born, they imagine that perhaps they might be fused through it. But the child is just another abandoned half, which soon rejects the first two trying to escape to find a fourth hemisphere. Such does not bode well for the "other half" theory.

Perhaps Cybèle was not his other half, but in their initial meeting, they had surely shared wavelengths. He'd been able to talk to her as to an old friend. He didn't have to come on in any way, just be himself. And he could see in her eyes she understood. And then, too, in some innocent way, she seemed to be aroused by him. The changing color of her skin. The intensified sparkle in her eyes. And then, working on Ravel! She'd grown ever more seductive, increasingly present to him, uncannily beautiful.

Well, he thought, that's what "in love" will give you. Why should he be indicted for having received such a gift? Why was he all of a sudden a purveyor of evil? She was a woman, not a child, a comfort, a balm, an escape, a break when he must surely need one. Angela was his, eternally, but the eternal has to know its place, which is not everywhere, all the time, forever. A rondo goes ABABABA, and rondo is the form we're in. At least he thought so. Does every moment have to be eternal? This thinking characterizes the male hemisphere.

The trouble, he thought, came from dishonesty. He would no longer be dishonest. He would confess his love to Cybèle, as he had confessed it to his wife. He suspected she knew, that her hesitation might just be fear of his love. He knew she was aware of him watching her at rehearsals, at mutual pauses, and during breaks. He would convince her there was nothing to fear. All out in the open. No one defrauded or betrayed.

Re: Bruce, the cat is already out of the bag: He, too, was in love with Cybèle. The problem was — he was supposed to be in love with someone else, or at least pretend to be.

He remembered precisely his first falling in love — at his childhood meeting with geometry, its sinuous working out of beautiful proofs which would stalk some truth like a cat a mouse, pounce, and snap it up in its jaws. It was a vision, a revelation of intellectual precision overpowering his senses, knocking him off his feet, and making his heart go pitty-pat.

He was amazed he could realize this dynamic with his brain, while his body remained entirely still, sitting at a table. His mind could expand, while his volume remained exactly the same. This, for some, is love.

All so-called "perfect beauty" — music, painting, a woman, or even his pouncing cat were just completions of their geometric figures, a circle, say, or an ellipse. The quality of that beauty was directly dependent on the shape completed, and the percentage of perimeter filled. Oval completers had completely different tones and effects than circular or square ones. Like a hologram, they each contained the complete essence of the figure they contained, and provoked the same emotions. Bruce was extremely partial to parabolas — "the locus of all points equidistant from a point and a line". Even the phrase "the locus of all points" was intoxicating to him, no matter the curve it defined. Whatever it was, it added a new dimension, an increase in reality, his alone among his blind, indifferent classmates.

Such was Cybèle for him — the locus of all points… he hesitated at the ellipsis. She was simply the locus of all points, period, the mirroring of reality at the instant of reality, reality come to shore. He got her, grokked her, knew her (not in the biblical sense, of course) with more than his brain, more than his heart, via more than anything he had learned or developed in life. He read her with more than his sight-reading skills. He read her with his childhood capacity for reality. Who needed a brain to be in love with Cybèle? Who needed intelligence? That's the way it was.

Needless to say it made his female-triangulation more difficult. In a room with both Angela and Cybèle (and when was it otherwise?) the isosceles triangle was extremely acute. But at least his and Cybèle's side were approaching one another. The smaller line A became, the closer the approximation of lines B and C. And this was also true in reality. Isn't math wonderful? Honest truth is the best policy.

———

Perimenopause is the time of life when periods become increasingly unpredictable before disappearing altogether. Estrogen goes down, testosterone goes up. Women often gain weight, though Angela had kept her spectacular figure. Perimenopause was often experienced as permanent PMS.

At Sekhmet, PMS was officially known as the Primal Mother Spell, as in "Oh, it's just the Primal Mother Spell." Some of the more waggish sisters knew PMS as Pissy Mood-, or even Part Monster-Syndrome. On the guest house refrigerator was posted a different cat from Bruce's Euclid, a particularly mean-looking, rumpled black beast staring over her left shoulder, announcing "I HAVE PMS AND A HANDGUN. ANY QUESTIONS?" It was held to the door by a magnetic button of a snarling cat face, with a circumferential slogan reading CLAWS BEAT SKIN.

Neither PM nor PMS was a particularly good time to go through what Angela was going through. Estrogen — that marvelous chemical that makes women want to help and serve, to cut up children's sandwiches in little squares — estrogen was in low supply, but could be supplemented topically and orally. Which Angela did. Neither was it a great time to be building a child, which Angela was doing, at present unaided by physicians.

Perhaps it was the effect of constant participation in Sekhmet support groups. Although Angela had experienced no acute traumas in life, though life in the main had flowed along, its challenges at the level of the Bach Chaconne, or a husband unfaithful in mind, if not in fact, she was beginning to experience a different truth entirely. She had to be honest: her life was a prison. The bars were musical, the locks were hairlike, the manacles partly mind-forged, but incarceration it was. Was she looking for apocalypse?

No. Then the most honest solution, paradoxically, was not to thrash her way to jailbreak, but to keep as still as possible, to minimize desire for alternatives, to refrain from asking questions. Give up her inner-tiger's tools. In imagining such a state, like the cosmic peace in Messiaen's *Liturgie de cristal*, the walls and bars began to retreat, and the world seemed to flow once again into her life, a wash of gratefully dancing tears.

She thought of her life with Peter, her long marriage. How she at first felt overpowered by another, more excellent being, as if living in his shadow. How strange, how dishonest even, that two alien lives pretend to fuse together even if, as now, they have a spiritually fitful connection. To be honest, their separateness was painfully clear, their coupledom slowly vanishing like evaporating fog.

Brought up by a rich family, subtly educated in pridefulness and beauty, she had assimilated an unstated elitism which had to disappear if all were to go well. Steeped in her Sekhmet milieu, she would try to fully embrace modesty, simplicity, deep connection with the earth and sky. Her prison would be dispelled. What could go wrong with that?

For Angela too, Cybèle was a complication. But her love for Cybèle could be the key to her escape from male dominance, male violence against women, even under the soft reign of Peter Warden, warden. "*Das Ewig-Weibliche zieht uns hinan*", yes! she thought. The Eternal Feminine would be the guide to drawing her *hinan* — onward, outward, upward.

⌁

Cybèle lay on her back on Sekhmet's skybed, nude, heavily sunscreened, under an explosive and trembling sun. Its fierce, shimmering heat engulfed her, and pummeled the inferno desert. Mesquite and cacti wobbled.

Some lines from Lamartine she had memorized at school flowed by in her head:

Midi, Roi des étés, épandu sur la plaine…

At this hour, she felt alone at the focal point of the universe, surrounded by a thousand square miles of no man's land, of no man's land.

Tout se tait. L'air flamboie et brûle sans haleine ;
La Terre est assoupie en sa robe de feu.

There were no premonitions of danger in this, her invulnerable universe.

Homme, si, le coeur plein de joie ou d'amertume,
Tu passais vers midi dans les champs radieux,
Fuis ! la Nature est vide et le Soleil consume :
Rien n'est vivant ici, rien n'est triste ou joyeux.

It's true she felt Peter and Bruce were acting weird
("*bizarre*", she thought), but then who in America
wasn't?

She let herself be drawn up into the vast desert sky.

Viens ! Le Soleil te parle en paroles sublimes ;
Dans sa flamme implacable absorbe-toi sans fin ;
Et retourne à pas lents vers les cités infimes,
Le coeur trempé sept fois dans le Néant divin.

She, who used to love flowers entwined in her
once-long chestnut hair. The only place to get them
was in the cemetery. The sisters caught her robbing
from the dead. There is nothing more abominable
than robbing from the dead, they said. She knew she
wasn't the first flower thief. She was suspended from
school — sent back to her brothers — for a week.
The little grave robber. "Let the dead bury the dead,"
they quoted. "Don't neglect the call Jesus gave you."
(Which command seemed irrelevant to her crime.)
"Let the spiritually dead attend to the routine tasks
of life." OK. Sure.

The bestial adolescent faces of her brothers were
those of the spiritually dead, and violating her seemed
to be one of their routine tasks in life. Their gift to her:
a repugnance for the act of love, an act, she felt, of
corruption and vice. She could not absolve them, she
could not make nothing out of their foul something,

she knew she was incapable of such a supernatural disappearing act.

She called on the sun to purify her angry soul. *Roi des étés.*

She had never really known what to do with her beauty. As an early adolescent, she would study herself in the mirror, starting with her hair. Without daring to do it, she would unbutton her reflection's dress, and let it fall to the floor. And she would study that image, right down to her lovely nails, fingers and toes, where her body would taper off into nothingness. Her innocent form. Still sinless.

Sometimes she thought she might really be wicked, as her brothers said she was. And that drove her into intolerable panic, and left her stranded and unhoused. Childish, serious as a child — but that's how children think.

At school, she'd waited uncertainly to become the real Cybèle. She was one of those impassioned young people who could hold herself motionless and reserved for a long time, but might then break down into total confusion, spirals that ran out of control, with the feelings of rage and deprivation which drove many of her peers to drinking, sex, and drugs. There, she had been protected by her brothers.

But now what to do about Angela? Hasty kisses

made her uncomfortable. Likewise whispered words of love. And although she had found a temporary home at Sekhmet, and had developed an unpredicted attachment to the Mojave, she was now, in her heart, an ex-pat.

And exile is a most difficult state, an unhealable schism between person and native place, between self and deep-rooted home. Literature, history, and biography contain many tales of heroic struggle overcoming exile. But such triumphs are likely seasoned by the loss of something forever left behind. She did not miss her brothers. She did not miss the hectoring sisters. But France, its lushness, and French, its beauty…she had to be honest. That, she missed. As Voltaire said, *"Quand la vérité met le poignard à la gorge, il faut baiser sa main blanche, quoique tachée de notre sang."*

A buzzing overhead. Cybèle knew it was not Martians escaped from the Area 51. And she was not about to have the boys in the trailers ogling over her nakedness.

⌁

Three drones down in one day? And the following week, two? Madman thought he had had the answer.

The Brit was right: When you have eliminated the impossible, whatever remains, however improbable, must be the truth. It was they, the three of them, the three longhairs with their lefty, peacenik schemes. How stupid he'd been. Sekhmet was the purloined letter, hiding under the obvious. That gaggle of banshees — the usual suspects — didn't even rank as improbable. And Angela had convinced her dupe husband to get the Captain on board, with his access to all the codes. One may smile and smile, and be a villain. I'll let them hang themselves with Dildo and the Anus, or whatever that Greek opera is they're cooking up. "Fight Violence Against Women Week." My boys will be at the performance. They'll be prepped. They think Creech is a prison? Wait till they get a load of a real one — from the inside. The jig, my friends, is up.

Fate Knocks

In fact,

What is it with Beethoven's Fifth? How did it worm its way into the Nevada desert? Cosmic dust storm? It isn't in the piano trio repertoire.

But they know it in the poolroom. They know it in the bar. They know it on the checkout line and at the beauty shop, at the garage and in the pizza joint. I'd wager even the spade foot toads croak it. Was there ever a phrase of music so embedded in our culture as the opening of Beethoven's Fifth? How come? How come it was the first symphony ever recorded, and how come Billy Joel said of da da da daaaa "it's one of the biggest hits in history — there's no video to it, but he didn't need one."?

Well, there is Schindler, Beethoven's friend, telling how the master pointed to the opening of the score and said, "This is fate knocking at the door." A good story, a plausible hook to hang one's interest on, especially with poor Ludwig going deaf, the symphony proceeding through the lyrical sadness of the second movement, past the weirdness of the Scherzo (Big Joke — on him), and emerging in C major at the end, blazing and triumphant. We'd like *that* to be our story — now more than ever. Unfortunately, there is lots of evidence that Schindler, like many authors, made the whole thing up. Besides, they don't know this story in the poolroom.

I have a theory: What is apparent is the uncanny power of those four tones, seeding every level of the work — themes, sections, movements, and the four movements as a whole — with their compressed energy. How might one characterize that energy?

Three short, fierce notes followed by a long note, held out of time. Then once again, a step lower, the long note held even longer. Goethe wrote a novel about elective affinities. But this theme, themelet, in time, out of time, short, long — this tiny seed theme asserts rather the contrast of Contraries. And to my mind, that is what B5 is "about" — the urgent confrontation and interaction of Contraries. And so are our lives, in the pool halls, in the trailers.

Yin and yang; despair and faith; awareness and blindness; deep and shallow; strong and weak; secular and sacred; earthly and ethereal; solid and hollow; visible and invisible; finite and infinite; noumena and phenomena; moving and still; changing and changeless; thrownness and purpose; light and dark; free and structured; serious and frivolous; work and play; celebration and despondence; peace and struggle; sorrow and joy; passion and intellect; inspiration and thought; simple and complex; lyric and dramatic; pure and impure; personal and im-; direct and oblique; free and imprisoned; improbable and expected; passive and aggressive; mind and body; nutritious and poisonous; exaggerated and understated; pompous and unassuming; closed and open; Apollo and Dionysis; organic and inorganic; love and hate; sensuous and ascetic; male and female; time and space; heaven and hell; life and death — Blake said "Without Contraries there is no progression." All pairs are implicit in the n-dimensional spiritual-emotional-philosophical space of Beethoven's Fifth, seeding its progression. Contraries, yin and yang, outbreath and inbreath at every level, and throughout. Though the first movement is the most compressed and extraordinary, Contraries haunt every movement.

Angela was reading *Howard's End* as a contrary to Don Quixote. There is a wonderful scene early on, at a performance of the Fifth. It is the transition between the Scherzo and the Finale — and the phenomenal reappearance of the Scherzo in the Finale which gives rise to some fascinating speculation on Contraries.

"Look out for the part where you think you have done with the goblins and they come back," one character whispers, as the Scherzo starts with goblins *"walking quietly over the universe, from end to end...They were not aggressive creatures; it was that that made them so terrible....They merely observed in passing that there was no such thing as splendor or heroism in the world."*

And then, at the end of the Scherzo, *"Beethoven took hold of the goblins and made them do what he wanted...He gave them a little push, and they began to walk in a major key instead of in a minor, and then — he blew with his mouth and they were scattered! Gusts of splendor..., magnificent victory."* Were the goblins not really there then? Were they just "phantoms of cowardice and unbelief?" Men like Theodore Roosevelt, Forster asserts, would say yes. But in the midst of the triumphant last movement, in one of the most surprising moments in music, escaped entirely from any traditional form, Beethoven brings them back.

"It was as if the splendor of life might boil over and waste to steam and froth. In its dissolution one heard the terrible, ominous note, and a goblin, with increased malignity, walked quietly over the universe from end to end. Panic and emptiness! Panic and emptiness! Even the flaming ramparts of the world might fail!

"Beethoven chose to make all right in the end… He blew with his mouth for a second time, and again the goblins were scattered. He brought back the gusts of splendor, the heroism, the youth, the magnificence of life and death, and, amid vast roarings of a superhuman joy, he led his Fifth Symphony to its conclusion. But the goblins were there. They could return. He had said so bravely, and that is why one can trust Beethoven when he says other things."

One might criticize Forster's "He blew with his mouth for a second time" for paucity of image, but "One can trust Beethoven" — that is the revealed truth. Truth will out. Honesty is the best policy. The opening of every movement of the Fifth says "Trust me." The mysterious da da da daaa of the Allegro, the strange and sad lyricism of the lower strings in the Andante, the What???! goblins of the Scherzo and the Back to Basics opening of the Finale — all are entirely convincing. All say "Trust me enough to give your entire self over." I think this explains the poolhall panache of da da da daaaa. For even this snippet, with its shrapnel Contrary, lodges itself deep in the psyche which knows that Contraries mean progression.

Ten ball in the side pocket. 4, 3, 2, 1...rifle!

DILDO AND THE ANUS

They needed something to bring them all together again, and the show was a go. Readers who began at the beginning will already know the result. Yet there were some interesting details along the way.

"Stop Violence Against Women Week" was to be nationally observed, with flags frequently lowered for all women killed by domestic violence. Federal money was available.

There had been some last minute debate among the four about the appropriateness of the Dido and Aeneas theme. Was it really violence against women? Was it feminist enough — with Dido dying just because her man left her? But her last aria convinced all that an act of great violence *had* been performed, a spiritual rape, some primal organ extracted against her will. Besides, it was the only somewhat relevant piece they could think of that they might actually be able to get together.

The Rev. Gen. Creech didn't need much convincing. He would get to see Angela again, perhaps even in a toga. Toga! Toga! And then, who knows what might follow? His boys might get some boots-on-the-ground action, and leave off grouching about the "prison" of their trailer shifts. And Inspector Javert would be afforded some extended observation of the likely culprits. Nothing surprising there.

Surprise number one was the resistance of the Sekhmet women to entertaining the enemy. Their world was so pleasant, so mutually supportive among themselves. Did they need to subject themselves to the leering commentary of construction workers times ten. Peter visited the Temple to drum up support, and invite auditions for singing roles, chorus, and silent, dancing crowds. It was the singing and dancing possibilities that turned the blood-dimmed tide. The consensus, finally, was that only art could triumph over violence, that Purcell's girls school was their own, that they, Didos all, needed to be remembered. It was true. Sort of. But it was a memorable evening. They would play the witches.

More surprising still was the reaction of Frank Murillo, Head of Security, the project's expected nemesis. An interview that began with "What now, Warden Warden?" was not promising. And the following "Another fucking intrusion into norms?" was par for the course. But as Peter told him the whats and whys of the show, a light seemed to dawn behind his bloodshot eyes."

"Say, listen up, I have an idea." He was becoming invested. "You know the Wiccans?"

Peter didn't know the Wiccans.

"How long have you been 'in charge of Programs', and you don't know the Wiccans? There's a secret cell of Wiccans here. Has been since the year after we opened."

"You mean in the Women's Unit?"

"Hell, no. Right here in C and D. Maybe a few guys in F. You think only women are witches?"

"And the Warden allows them to...practice?"

"He has to. Nevada Supreme Court ruling, affirmed by the Federal Appeals Court. Wicca is a bona fide religious belief entitled to protection under the First Amendment. Of course, they have to be sincere, and practice the beliefs in their daily lives."

"What do they do?"

"Oh, you know. Serious chanting — spells to improve prison conditions. They say their own blue work shirts represent esoteric knowledge. They write the names of demons on scraps of paper and burn them. Like that."

"Are they sincere?"

"Of course not. They do it to rag on us and get some club time. After the court order, Straud, in his transcendent tolerance, even bequeathed a miserable patch of dirt for them in the yard for Wiccan gatherings. You may have seen that little enclosure at the north end. Wiccan ground zero. They planted a pentacle made of contraband metal."

"Do they ... gather around it?"

"You haven't seen them? They look just like all the other cons, hanging out, jawing. A bunch of your classic pimpled, white late-teen Trekkie-types, except they're in for robbery, rape, one for murder. They've planted a few things there in the Wiccan sacred soil. Brown things. Like the mesquite growing everywhere else but theirs is somehow more cancer-like, stunted, twisted..."

"What do they say about what they're doing, about Wicca?"

"What do you think? They never tell you what their 'religion' is all about, other than some vague references to nature, the seasons, the moon, the goddess."

"They worship goddesses?"

"Sure. When they're not beating the shit out of them. They'll tell you what they are not, like devil-worshippers and definitely not Christians."

"Amazing."

"Yeah. They might love to play witches in your musical. It'd be our revenge for all their shucking."

"The witches are already taken, but they could play sailors, victims of the witches."

"Victims. Yeah, I think they'd like that. That's their fallback."

And so, they were cast — at least in Peter's head. It would take a bit of convincing.

But the biggest surprise of all was the decision for the quartet — all of them — to themselves take on the major roles. The original notion had been for the prisoners alone to do the show — a men's version of the schoolgirl opera — rehearsed in Peter's theater group, and attended by selected sociopaths from Creech. Anything else would be more complicated, requiring prison passes, extra security, and body searches for civilians entering and leaving.

But the enthusiasm of the Sekhmet women to take part, and the relative ease of training a women's chorus in women's choruses, changed the whole picture, and opened it up to other possibilities. And when soloists who could handle the title roles could not be found, the final die was cast: Angela would sing Dido, though her last vocalizing was long past. Peter would sing Aeneas, though his excellence on cello was not necessarily transferrable to voice. Still, he was a wonderful musician, and had learned acting skills, if only in his own workshops. Cybèle would play Belinda, Dido's court companion and friend. For was this not really the case? And they all knew she could handle the difficult part. The Captain, would, of course play piano, the battered old upright which Peter would have tuned for the occasion.

Rehearsals chez Warden were rich with subtext. While Peter was Anglea's lover, committed to her longterm, he was being wooed by other voices, other commands. Leaving their marriage, a Triumph of Love and Beauty, though never before imagined, was not beyond the realm of thought. *Fear no danger to ensue, the Hero loves as well as you?* Much was suspicious between them as their Purcell personae vowed eternal love.

The Hero loves as well as you? Did Angela still love? Of course, but too widely. She loved Cybèle just as much as Peter, and that "just as much" was delicately balanced with "if not more". While her initial reaction to Peter's confession was hardly Dido's steadfast rejection of a commitment with someone who had even thought of leaving, much less love for another. Still, calling him a "deceitful Crocodile" was overstating the case. She felt moved to protect him against the ravings of her own character. And the continual intimate attentions from Belinda only made that more difficult.

Was she ready to die? No. For love of a man? No. That would never pass muster at Sekhmet. Would Cybèle be upset if she died? She'd love to know, but there might be other ways than death to find out.

And then there was the baby. Dido was not pregnant by Aeneas. Or at least no one was saying. But this Dido? Did she want to live for the baby? His baby? Ironic monument to a collapsed world? They had arranged for a home birth with the two midwives currently in residence at the Temple. Much wisdom there, for sure, but it was still not too late to abort. What about that?

And when would she start to show? Though it might be post-modernly poignant, it really wouldn't do for Aeneas to abandon a gravid queen — though a million-dollar idea, there, for the next punk production of *Dido*. But not at the prison, in a program promoting respect for morality, not in front of young military studs who leave enough orphans already.

Cybèle's scenes with her mistress and queen were emotionally compromised by her knowledge that both the pianist and the hero were following her every move. Eyes, certainly, and probably with hearts. She felt guilty for distracting their attentions — onstage

258

from the queen, and offstage from husband and friend. *Fear no Danger to ensue, the Hero loves as well as you?* Yes, but he loved *her*, Cybèle, and quite a bit of Danger there for all, including, she realized, herself.

The Sekhmet women were no problem. Thought they'd be loathe to admit it, the role of witches suited them to a T. T for tit. T for tittilate. *In our deep vaulted Cell we'll prepare*, they'd sing, *too dreadful a Practice for this open Air. Harm's our Delight and Mischief all our Skill…*Who would think these thoughtful, educated women, full of political analysis would be so convincing? And the *Ho, ho, ho, ho* laughing choruses sounded a lot more like *Hee, hee, hee, hee*, with no Purcell indication for cackling.

The prisoners took a little more dealing with, but this was Peter's idea, and he took responsibility for doing so. The Wiccans, as expected, wanted to be witches. Peter convinced them that to maintain their yard cred, it would be better not to fly Purcell's flag. All right, they would be sailors with the other men. Singing *Come away, fellow Sailors, your Anchors be weighing* was difficult for them, as it would be for a quadriplegic to sing *Sing we and dance it*. But Peter's talk on rain dances and victimhood magic convinced them. Besides, they'd up their chances with the Parole Board by participating. The Witches didn't know it yet, nor did they, but each of these two groups would present a distinct threat to the other. And a matchless opportunity.

Those readers who've read from the beginning, already know what happened. Though it didn't end properly, it was actually one of the great performances of *Dido*. Both Angela and Cybèle were in top form, heightened by nervousness, but deeply in touch with their respective inner torments. Peter, too, while not being as vocally adept, realized his prison rep and prisoner programs, and possibly even his job, were riding on the evening's success. Lots of warmup that night, and the kind of practice he hadn't put in since his principal cellist days at Berkeley. Bruce, as usual, was spectacular, and treated his clunker keyboard as a *Mahagonny* vessel of *ewige Kunst*.

The walled-off section of the gym was packed with prisoners, staff, airmen, officers, and a contingent of civilians who didn't mind submitting to entrance and exit body searches. The music critic from the *Sun* was there, and the Lt. Governor and his wife and children, all the way down from Carson City. The gym had been chosen over the cafeteria because Warden Stroud thought ceramic and plastic could more easily become missiles than the locked-down iron should anything untoward occur.

Stroud mounted the shop-built platform, introduced Peter to the assembled crowd. Peter, overcoat over costume, introduced the military visitors, spoke about their shared Violence Against Women project, told some of the history of Purcell's piece, and thanked the Warden for his permission to perform, and his progressive attitude concerning corrections. High Desert, he said, was coming to be seen nationally as a leader in prison reform, and tonight's evening would prove it.

The reporters took notes, the politicians smiled electoral smiles, and the Creechies, as instructed, made sure their iCameras were on and their ringers turned off.

"And now, without further ado..." Peter whipped "off-stage" behind a 4X8 proscenium wall.

As we know, there was much further ado.

Coping

Bruce's burial was paid for by the Department of Defense. His service was conducted by his commander, The Rev. Gen. William Creech III on a text from Ecclesiastes. The trio of guilty survivors had no reason to suspect him of anything other than being himself. Under the Captain's crossed coffin-hands they placed a copy of the Chopin Second sonata, a piece the composer might have played on his Pleyel. It wasn't exactly an example of "Even Beauty must die," but it was tragic nonetheless.

This is the little speech Peter made at the grave. He attributed to Bruce a vision of sunlit transparency which could always be heard in his playing. His life had been dedicated not to unmanned aerial vehicles, but to finding or creating real human beings at their controls. He gave to Bruce's vision the language of Milton, a world in which

> *speckled vanity*
> *will sicken and soon die,*

And leprous sin will
melt from earthly mould
and Hell itself will pass away
and leave her dolorous mansion
to the peering day.

Nice touch, nice try. It was a hit. Some mourners may have wept.

Harder, though, was coping with Partner Rape. It's bad enough when your partner rapes you, but it involves other issues entirely when it is your partner who is raped. Shock and depression, of course, and a sense of betrayal by men he trusted in the face of Murillo's warnings. But harder to live with was his irrational sense that both his loves, both Angela and Cybèle, were now polluted. Sperm may have flowed that evening, but not into or even onto them. What had some prisoners' lust had to do with those poor women? And it was not just the dueling erections that bothered him. It was the violence that flowed, and who else but his women the proximal cause?

Both the women were afterwards depressed — and also anxious, jittery, fearful of nothing and everything. Angela bordered on hysteria; Cybèle felt frozen, and acted dead. Both refused to discuss the evening. Both thought maybe they should move.

Their feelings, too, were beyond rational. What

was the difference between the prison happening, and being at a police riot — which Angela had experienced in Berkeley, and Cybèle had witnessed visiting a friend in Toulouse? Those whose role was violence would leave violence in their wake, and that role was not theirs. Still, they each in their way, Protestant and Catholic, felt guilty, and yes, polluted. They would not, could not, see the larger context of systemic repression overcome, of seething class and race issues, of plain old, rudderless hellionism. With the myopia of solipsism, they thought the whole affair was related to *them*, that they had "come on" in various ways. Rending their garments? What sane woman would do that in an audience of military and prisoners? Why had they followed Peter into the trap? In the name of Art? Therapy? In the name of Institutional Progress?

Alienation was increased all around. Peter, Angela and Cybèle examined each other and their lives, and found them all wanting.

A Child Is Born

How was a child to be born under such circumstances? With some difficulty. The uterine muscles of a perimenopausal mom have lost some enthusiasm for contraction, and with midwives in Nevada not licensed to administer pitocin, the labor can be long, even with Sekhmet massage and incantations. Then too, older mothers are at greater risk of giving birth to children with genetic abnormalities. Encouraged by the Sekhmet vibe to refuse ultrasound and amniocentesis, Angela would take what came, boy or girl or whatever else.

Older eggs sometimes get sloppy with meiosis, and can contain an extra chromosome. A baby born from such an egg may wind up with that unasked-for guest crashing in every cell. More is not better. The most common condition to result is called trisomy 21, Down syndrome, a third 21st chromosome, instead of the normal two.

But aging Angela remained a rare bird. The baby

had brought down from his oddball egg a condition of trisomy 8, thankfully mosaicised — two populations of cells in the same child, some normal, some trisomic — due to another (saving) complication in mitosis.

Whereas complete trisomy 8 is usually fatal, trisomy 8 mosaics show a milder range of problems, and T8 babies are more likely to survive to adulthood, albeit with psychomotor difficulties, moderate-to-severe retardation, abnormal height one way or the other. Their faces can be expressionless, and they often show odd and unpredictable physical abnormalities. The type and severity of symptoms depend on the sites and proportion of normal and trisomic cells.

Deep creases in palms and feet are considered pathognomic, especially in combination with thick lips, pinky-flexion, and hip abnormalities, and these were the first things the midwives noted as they inventoried infant Warden's parts. They had to look them up in their perinatal symptoms guide.

His future? Hopeful, but who knows? Let it be, let it be. It could have been worse.

Perhaps, as Marilyn Manson said, "Music is the strongest form of magic." But on the other hand, Angela was too far-gone to undertake motherhood — especially of a "special" child. It seemed truly, wildly, beyond her. Emotionally exhausted before the current crisis, she was now completely distraught. And Peter was completely distraught. Some potential parents.

In late December, as part of their Christmas season, the First Baptist Church of Indian Springs held a memorial service for their late organist and music director, Bruce Fiedler Boynton.

Combining both occasions, Peter, Angela and Cybèle decided to perform Brahms' lovely spiritual lullaby, his *Geistliches Wiegenlied*, arranged by Peter for their particular trio, luckily excluding the church piano. It would take only one rehearsal from musicians of their caliber.

At one point Cybèle, channeling Mary, sang a lovely cadential phrase, imploring the trees to hush their rustling so her child may sleep: *Stillet die Wipfel — es schlummert mein Kind, es schlummert mein Kind*. Angela stopped her playing, and so Peter stopped his. Cybèle looked at them quizzically.

"What is wrong?" she asked.

"You want a baby?" Angela responded.

"What?"

"I said, 'Do you want a baby?"

"With who?" Cybèle, shocked, inquired.

"With me. I mean from me. Do you want baby Bruce?"

"Angela…" said her husband, holding up his bow to stop her.

"I'm serious. I can't do it. We can't do it. It's not fair to him. He'll need parents who aren't messed up the way we are, parents with more, with clearer energy, who won't be old people he'll be ashamed of in fourth grade…if he gets to fourth grade."

"Angela, this isn't…"

"I'm just asking, Peter. When she sang *es schlummert mein Kind*, she seemed so right."

"She's just a beautiful singer. She doesn't want a baby."

"Your baby."

"OK, she doesn't want my baby. We have enough complications as it is."

"Cybèle?" Angela asked.

Cybèle, silent, heard all these things and pondered them in her heart. Such an *adoption informal* was perhaps the answer, the unique answer. She could have a child without intercourse or spreading her legs for white-coated male doctors. Too often had she played patient as her brothers played doctor. She could be Peter's partner without being his bedmate, and Angela's, without falling into sin. Her raising baby Bruce would be an act of *caritas* the sisters would be proud of, and would pay an unthreatening *hommage* to that strange genius man who, distressingly, had fallen in love with the wrong person. So much potential in that off-beat little infant.

In recognition of her changed status, Cybèle was relocated at Sehkmet. In a touching ritual with flutes, cymbals and drums, she was moved from the Maiden Room to the Mother Room, and in it, she often sat of an evening singing to her child.

> *Do-do, l'en-fant do*
> *L'enfant dor-mir-a bien vite,*
> *Do-do, l'enf-ant do*
> *L'enfant dor-mir-a bientôt.*

Postlude In Heaven

The Masters, smoking and drinking, watched the screen even more intently than before. On hearing Cybèle's lullaby, Goethe remarked, *"Schön. Aber kein* Kinderetotenlied." Mahler tipped his Zylinder. "I vill use it in ze Tenth." "Jah, jah, jah," Brecht said, sighing.

"*¡Alégrense, señores!*" Cervantes, ever cheerful.

And cheer up they did when Brecht began quietly singing, almost as commentary,

Denn wie man sich bettet, so liegt man

The tune was picked up by Goethe:

Es deckt einen da keiner zu

Now more jaunty, joined by Mahler:

Und wenn einer tritt, dann bin ich es

And finally, the whole quartet, energetic:

Und wird einer getreten, dann bist's du.

Repeat, tutti:

Denn wie man sich bettet, so liegt man

Es deckt einen da keiner zu
Und wenn einer tritt, dann bin ich es
Und wird einer getreten, dann bist's du.

Cervantes got his turn.
Como haces tu cama, dormirás.
Nadie va a hacerla por ti,
Y si alguien te pega, es que soy yo.
Y si es pegado, serás tú.

And as simultaneously translated, intercepted by homeland security,
As you make your bed, you must lie there,
There ain't no housekeeping crew,
And if someone's to kick, then I'll do that,
And if someone gets kicked, then that's you.

Singing grandly, bawling at the top of their lungs, cigars and steins in hand, they marched around the heavenly poolroom.

THE MUSIC IN SPECKLED VANITIES

Purcell

"Great Minds Against Themselves Conspire" from his opera, *Dido and Aeneas*

https://www.youtube.com/watch?v=haE-pvDif4s

Purcell

"When I am laid in Earth, may my Wrongs create no Trouble in thy Breast" from *Dido and Aeneas*

https://www.youtube.com/watch?v=1S_84N0V81U

Morley

Canzonet: "Do You Not Know" ("Shee with her beauty blazing...")

www.youtube.com/watch?v=yJPSVQxsrKU

Mendelssohn

Piano Trio in D minor, op 49, first movement

https://www.youtube.com/watch?v=5J8ie4uYJ6M

Schubert

Piano Trio in B♭: movement two

https://www.youtube.com/watch?v=hGSvcnQ7J20

Bach

Fugue from Sonata #3 for Unaccompanied Violin

https://www.youtube.com/watch?v=RG7rx3BO6JY

Bloch

Suite for Unaccompanied Violin

https://www.youtube.com/watch?v=VoaZs_1OjDE

Bartok

Sonata for Unaccompanied Violin (fugue is 2nd
movement, beginning at 13:16)

https://www.youtube.com/watch?v=qKnggsxx2II

Bach

Chaconne from the Partita #2 for Unaccompanied
Violin

https://www.youtube.com/watch?v=myXOrVv-fNk

Ravel

Sonata for Violin and Cello

https://www.youtube.com/watch?v=xDKLJiGt5Hs

Scarlatti

Sonata in G major

https://www.youtube.com/watch?v=ynaJ2R24zDU

Bach

C# minor fugue from the *Well-Tempered Clavier*

https://www.youtube.com/watch?v=vHn4lfXEG9k

Beethoven

Fugue from the *Hammerklavier Sonata*

https://www.youtube.com/watch?v=yRDcgjvjj2E

Brahms

Intermezzo in A major

https://www.youtube.com/watch?v=1h4Re5WBEAc

Beethoven

Violin Sonata # 9 ("Kreutzer") Movement #2

https://www.youtube.com/watch?v=BE52VxCfqaw

Josquin des Pres

Ave Maria

https://www.youtube.com/watch?v=Xt3H2uGxFLI

Kurt Weill

"Wir brauchen keinen Hurikan" from the opera,
Mahagonny

https://www.youtube.com/watch?v=FA6NXiSkqHA
(begins at 4:13)

Schumann
"Ein Jüngling liebt ein Mädchen" from the song
cycle *Dichterliebe*
https://www.youtube.com/watch?v=lOIWebk1jco

Ravel
"Nahandove", the first song in his *Chansons
Madecasses*
https://www.youtube.com/watch?v=qHoSLEKux10

Purcell
"In our deep vaulted cell" from *Dido and Aeneas*
https://www.youtube.com/watch?v=G-swJMp_NwM

Purcell
"Harm's our Delight and Mischief all our Skill"
from *Dido and Aeneas*
https://www.youtube.com/watch?v=qGoWqyrWah8

Purcell
"Ho, ho, ho, ho" from *Dido and Aeneas* (3:35)
https://www.youtube.com/watch?v=lMUnMSdA4u0

Purcell
"Come away, fellow sailors" from *Dido and Aeneas*
https://www.youtube.com/watch?v=qdtrCmnVNdw

Kurt Weill

"Das ist die ewige Kunst" piano solo from
Mahagonny (until 1:30)

https://www.youtube.com/watch?v=aEHQsgXUGN8

Brahms

Geistliches Wiegenlied

https://www.youtube.com/watch?v=H48SBId3CMQ

French lullaby

"Do-do, l'en-fant do"

https://www.youtube.com/watch?v=ioLM0Ig4hFI

Kurt Weil

"Denn wie man sich bettet, so liegt man" from
Mahagonny (begins as 0:53)

https://www.youtube.com/watch?v=GxTu9CA7zW4

Thanks

to Peter Seidenberg, April Johnson, John Dunlop, and Laura Markowitz for tips on what cellist/violinist couples do for fun,

to Tim Guiles for considerations in buying a grand piano,

to Tina Escaja for Cervantization of Brecht,

to Katticus Metallicus for the skinny on tramp stamps,

to Kit Andrews and John Gorczyk for professional takes on prisons,

to The Pierson Library Book Club for its critical look at, and suggestions for, the manuscript: Carol Casey, Connie Bonaccio, Carol Kogut, Judith and Hans Puck,

to Bill Metcalf's choral programming for bringing the Milton Ode to my attention for title, epigraph, and eulogy.

AND THANKS IN ADVANCE to any reader posting his or her thoughts about the book online. This is a new double-direction for writers and their readers, and a corrective to the shrinking of book review space in the mass media. Writing reviews on Amazon, Barnes & Noble, Facebook, Goodreads, Shelfari, Library Thing or other social media sites help the progress of independent publishing.

Fomite

A fomite is a medium capable of transmitting infectious organisms from one individual to another.

"The activity of art is based on the capacity of people to be infected by the feelings of others." Tolstoy, *What Is Art?*

Writing a review on Amazon, Good Reads, Shelfari, Library Thing or other social media sites for readers will help the progress of independent publishing. To submit a review, go to the book page on any of the sites and follow the links for reviews. Books from independent presses rely on reader to reader communications.

For more information or to order any of our books, visit http://www.fomitepress.com/FOMITE/Our_Books.html

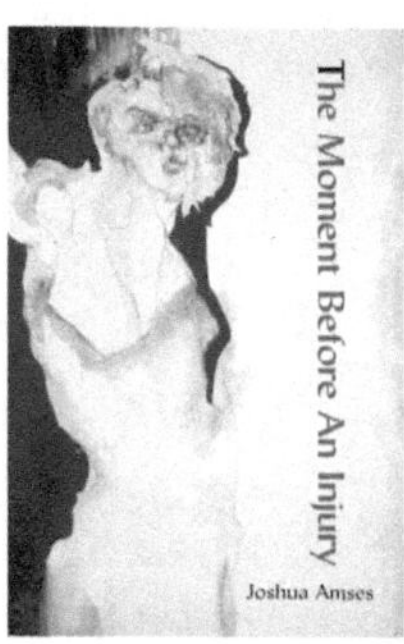

The Moment Before an Injury
Joshua Amses

Nothing Beside Remains
Jaysinh Birjépatil

The Way None of This Happened
Mike Breiner

Victor Rand
David Brizer

Summer on the Cold War Planet
Paula Closson Buck

Cycling in Plato's Cave
David Cavanagh

Fomite

Where There Are Two or More
Elizabeth Genovise

The Hundred Yard Dash Man
Barry Goldensohn

When You Remeber Deir Yassin
R. L. Green

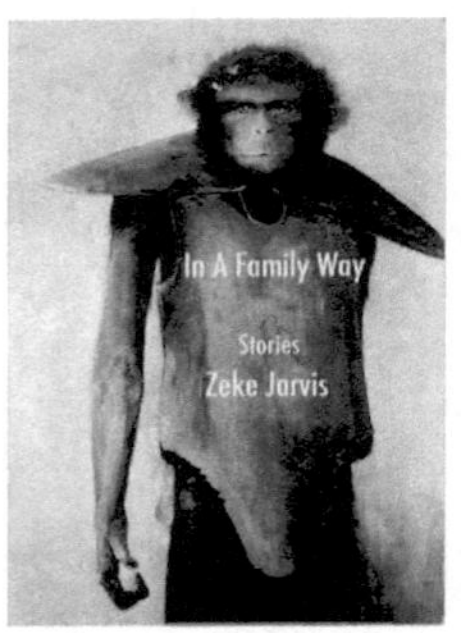

In A Family Way
Zeke Jarvis

A Free, Unsullied Land
Maggie Kast

Feminist on Fire
Coleen Kearon

Thicker Than Blood
Jan English Leary

A Guide to the Western Slope
Roger Lebovitz

Confessions of a Carnivore
Diane Lefer

*Unborn Children of
America*
Michele Markarian

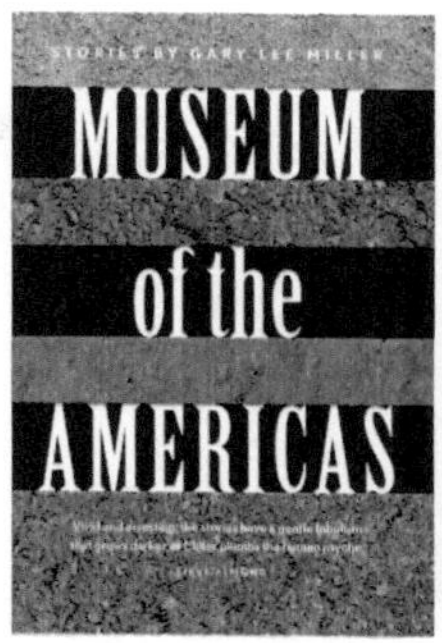

*Museum of the
Americas*
Gary Lee Miller

My Father's Keeper
Andrew Potok

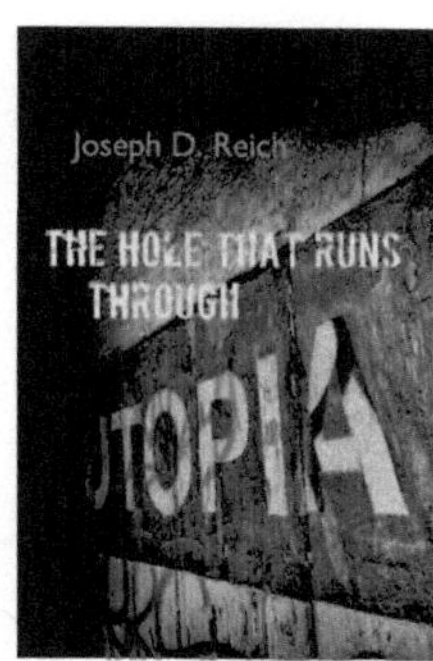

*The Hole That Runs
Through Utopia*
Joseph D. Reich

Companion Plants
Kathryn Roberts

Rafi's World
Fred Russell

*My Murder
and Other Local News*
David Schein

*Planet Kasper
Volume Two*
Peter Schumann

Bread & Sentences
Peter Schumann

Fomite

Industrial Oz
Scott T. Starbuck

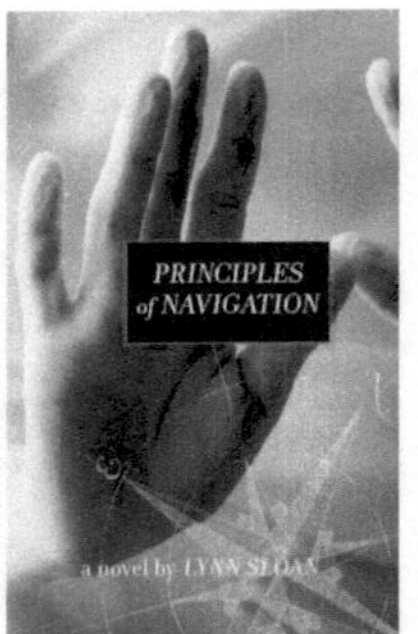

Principles of Navigation
Lynn Sloan

Among Angelic Orders
Susan Thoma

Everyone Lives Here
Sharon Webster

The Falkland Quartet
Tony Whedon

*The Return of
Jason Green*
Suzi Wizowaty

*The Inconveniece
of the Wings*
Silas Dent Zobal

Fomite

More Titles from Fomite...

Joshua Amses — *Raven or Crow*

Joshua Amses — *The Moment Before an Injury*

Jaysinh Birjepatil — *The Good Muslim of Jackson Heights*

Antonello Borra — *Alfabestiario*

Antonello Borra — *AlphaBetaBestiario*

Jay Boyer — *Flight*

Dan Chodorkoff — *Loisada*

Michael Cocchiarale — *Still Time*

Greg Delanty — *Loosestrife*

Zdravka Evtimova — *Carts and Other Stories*

Anna Faktorovich — *Improvisational Arguments*

Derek Furr — *Suite for Three Voices*

Stephen Goldberg — *Screwed*

Barry Goldensohn — *The Listener Aspires to the Condition of Music*

Greg Guma — *Dons of Time*

Andrei Guruianu — *Body of Work*

Ron Jacobs — *The Co-Conspirator's Tale*

Ron Jacobs — *Short Order Frame Up*

Ron Jacobs — *All the Sinners Saints*

Kate MaGill — *Roadworthy Creature, Roadworthy Craft*

Ilan Mochari — *Zinsky the Obscure*

Fomite

Jennifer Moses — *Visiting Hours*

Sherry Olson — *Four-Way Stop*

Janice Miller Potter — *Meanwell*

Jack Pulaski — *Love's Labours*

Charles Rafferty — *Saturday Night at Magellan's*

Joseph D. Reich — *The Derivation of Cowboys & Indians*

Joseph D. Reich — *The Housing Market*

Fred Russell — *Rafi's World*

Peter Schumann — *Planet Kasper, Volume 1*

L. E. Smith — *The Consequence of Gesture*

L. E. Smith — *Travers' Inferno*

L. E. Smith — *Views Cost Extra*

Susan Thomas — *The Empty Notebook Interrogates Itself*

Tom Walker — *Signed Confessions*

Susan V. Weiss — *My God, What Have We Done?*

Peter Mathiessen Wheelwright — *As It Is On Earth*